———————————— ★ ————————————

"The murder instrument was a marble replica of Michelangelo's David, about a foot high, the kind so many tourists bring back from Florence. It was found on the dresser, and items in the bottom dresser drawer seem to have been used to wipe bloodstains from his hands."

"You keep saying he and him and his."

"There is a partial footprint in some spilled talcum. A man's shoe."

"A thief who did not steal and who apparently killed without premeditation?"

Katherine nodded. "The police will of course be speaking to Gregory Doyle. Do you think him capable of such a deed?"

Sister Dempsey's eyes rounded. "I think anyone is capable of any deed in certain circumstances. It will be discovered that he was much provoked by his wife."

———————————— ★ ————————————

"[Mary Teresa's] character has been likened to Agatha Christie's Miss Marple..."
                                    —*Arizona Daily Star*

MONICA QUILL

Nun Plussed

WORLDWIDE®

TORONTO • NEW YORK • LONDON
AMSTERDAM • PARIS • SYDNEY • HAMBURG
STOCKHOLM • ATHENS • TOKYO • MILAN
MADRID • WARSAW • BUDAPEST • AUCKLAND

NUN PLUSSED

A Worldwide Mystery/December 1995

First published by St. Martin's Press, Incorporated.

ISBN 0-373-26187-X

Printed in U.S.A.

Nun Plussed

ONE

It was Sister Mary Teresa Dempsey's practice to read her mail in the study after breakfast, reserving table time for chatting with Sisters Kimberly and Joyce. The three of them were the remnant of the Order of Martha and Mary that had once flourished in Chicago, their college west of the city providing an excellent liberal education and what in an early time had been called "finishing" for young women. It was there that Emtee Dempsey had taught history, it was from there to this house on Walton Street that she had withdrawn when a majority of her sisters, misinterpreting Vatican II, had renewed the order almost out of existence.

The ecumenical council had urged religious women to seek new and appropriate ways of living their vocation in the modern world. For too many, this meant adopting the outlook of the world. Habits were changed—habits of behavior as well as of dress. Hundreds left the convent. This house, designed by Frank Lloyd Wright, the gift of a grateful alumna, together with lake property near Michigan City, Indiana, was all that was left of a once prosperous and flourishing community. The college had been sold off, the proceeds frittered away, and members of the order drifted into the world.

One adjusted to circumstances so long as one did not compromise one's principles. The regime of the house on Wanton Street hewed as closely as its numbers permitted to the traditional horarium set forth by the Blessed Abigail Keineswegs almost two centuries before, when she founded the Order of Martha and Mary. Sister Mary Teresa might have sat and wept over Babylon for the rest of her days, living in the past, her whole life a statement of I-told-you-so. But this was not in Emtee Dempsey's nature. She went on with her scholarly work as before. Kim was likely to follow in her footsteps; Joyce kept the house running smoothly. The rule's injunction to reserve mealtime "for pleasant and edifying conversation with the sisters" precluded reading mail at the breakfast table. Emtee Dempsey, despite her eagerness to read a letter she had seen in the morning's mail, lingered over a second cup of coffee.

When she did withdraw to her study, only moments went by before a wailing was heard. Kim, her heart in her throat, hurried down the hall and into the study. She half feared to find the elderly nun gasping her last. Instead she found her moving back and forth in the room, using her cane to punish the floor rather than assist her progress.

"What is it?"

Wordlessly, the old nun held out a letter, dramatically turning away as she did so.

It was a wedding invitation. Margaret Nelson Doyle announced her coming marriage to Philip Chesney Cord. The ceremony was to be held in a Methodist church in Berwyn. The names meant nothing to Kim.

"Is she an alumna?"

"Yes! And her mother before her."

Therefore, presumably, Catholic. For Margaret Nelson Doyle to be married in a Methodist ceremony obviously suggested apostasy to the old nun.

"Sister, mixed marriages are sometimes performed in Protestant churches, with both a priest and the minister presiding."

"Oh, if only it were so simple."

"What's complicated?"

"Margaret Nelson *Doyle*. She is already married."

Kim felt she was reporting on the general decadence of the time when she reminded Emtee Dempsey of the ease with which annulments are now obtained. For all they knew, in the eyes of the Church this would be her first marriage.

"For that matter, Mr. Doyle could be dead."

"If he is I have been dealing with a ghost."

Doyle? Kim needed only a moment's thought.

"The bookseller?"

The old nun's nod caused the great traditional headdress she wore to make movements as if preparatory to lifting her from the ground. The habit worn from the time of the Blessed Abigail until the depredations of the postcouncil, the habit Emtee Dempsey had donned as a young girl, she continued to wear. Others might choose not to walk faithfully in the vocation to which they were called, but she had given her heart and soul to the Lord when she took her religious vows, and with his grace she intended to remain true to them until she died.

"Of course I cannot attend."

"I doubt she expects that."

"No, not that. What she wants is my approbation. She puts me in an impossible position. Either I hold to my principles, refuse to recognize this second marriage, and run the risk of looking like a righteous pharisee, or I forfeit my principles, give her my blessing, and make a mockery of my beliefs."

Kim thought Emtee Dempsey might be overstating the role she was being cast for. Not all alumnae had accepted their former teacher as their main mentor in life. It was conceivable that an invitation had been sent to Wanton Street without any of the complications the old nun saw even entering Margaret Nelson Doyle's mind.

"I don't think I know her."

"That's another thing. Why is she getting married again at her age?"

This was not a rhetorical question. Sister Mary Teresa proceeded to develop a theory to explain why a woman in her mid-forties was abandoning her first husband and taking another. The Fountain of Youth that Ponce de Leon allegedly sought in Florida was now sought at the altar. By contracting marriage after marriage, men and women tried to return to the beginning of life, to start over. To be young again.

"The surest sign of maturity, Sister Kimberly, is to accept the age one is. That seems trivial, but you will find upon reflection that an infallible mark of maturity is a person's acceptance of who they are. Self-identity cannot ignore the date of one's birth."

This might have been boasting, since few septuagenarians of Kim's acquaintance accepted their age as emphatically as Emtee Dempsey.

"It is said that seventy-seven is no longer old. What is meant is that one's life expectancy is greater. Seventy-seven nonetheless *is* old. It is also a glorious age."

That the old nun went on so long about the wedding invitation indicated how close she still felt to all those young women who had been educated in the order's college, with particular reference of course to former students of her own.

"Margaret is an extraordinarily gifted woman. She always was."

"Was there ever a student of the college that was other than exceptional?"

"Oh my, yes. During its last years—"

"Thanks a lot."

Bright blue eyes appeared above the rimless spectacles. "Don't fish for compliments, Sister."

"What were her gifts?"

"Languages. And not just the syntactical and grammatical surface. She could get swiftly into another culture thanks to her mastery of modern languages."

"Did she do graduate work?"

"No. She met Gregory Doyle."

Kim had met the bookseller. Actually, he was far more than that: He also did binding and restoration work on old books. He was a man with whom Emtee Dempsey often had dealings. Invariably when Doyle found something irresistible, Mr. Rush, the order's lawyer, a contemporary of Emtee Dempsey and a former trustee of the college, came up with the money for the purchase. It had been a dark day in Emtee Dempsey's life when she began to find books from the college library on the shelves of used book dealers in the Chicago area. One of her purchases, thanks to Mr. Rush, had been the college's set of

Muratori and the Rolls series, indispensable documentation for Italian and English history.

"I enlisted Margaret's husband to track down whatever of worth showed up. Much of what we had was standard stuff, no great loss, though I shall never reconcile myself to the iconoclastic zeal with which one generation of the order sold off the accumulated accomplishments of previous generations of women. I stopped Mr. Rush from seeking a court order to put an end to it, fearing to create scandal. It was bad enough that a religious order was seeking to put itself out of business. Calling public attention to it would only have been worse."

"Were they partners?"

"In the business? No." She considered her next remark. "It would have been better if they had been."

"What does she do?"

"Until recently, she raised her children, two boys and a girl. What must they make of this?" She lifted the wedding invitation and let it drop upon her desk. "The girl married just last summer."

"How do you keep all these things straight?"

Emtee Dempsey did not understand the question. She was speaking of her former students and their families and would not have thought remembering the details of their lives amounted to some feat of memory.

Joyce came in to tell Emtee Dempsey that she would be serving their luncheon guest *riz provençal*, brochettes of lamb, and green beans. Dessert would be custard.

"Guest?"

Joyce looked at Kim. "It *is* today, isn't it?"

"Geoffrey Stone, Sister. About your Newberry Lecture."

Her frown gave way to a smile. "Oh, good. All these distractions have taken their toll."

But the distractions were just beginning. Kim went upstairs to her room to work, since she was expected to be at table when Sister Emtee Dempsey entertained Geoffrey Stone. Before settling down, she switched on WBBM, five minutes of which at any hour of the day gave her more news than she cared to have.

It was uncannily like an old movie, in which a turned-on radio fits right into the ongoing action: A prominent Chicago woman had been found slain in her home within the hour. The body of Mrs. Margaret Nelson Doyle had been discovered by her daughter. Apparently the victim surprised an intruder. Further details were promised.

Kim switched off the radio. She wished she had not turned it on, as if not knowing the dreadful news would cancel it. For much of the morning Kim had been hearing good and bad things about this woman,

who might have been dying even as she was being
discussed on Walton Street.

There were two things she could do, after having
breathed a prayer for the poor woman's soul. First,
she could telephone Katherine and see what their old
friend might know, or, second, she could go right
downstairs and tell Sister Mary Teresa.

She met Joyce on the stairs.

"What's the matter?"

"Is it that obvious?"

"Tell me."

"Come with me when I tell Sister."

It seemed a time when their diminutive community of three should be together.

TWO

SHE HAD BEEN NAMED Bernadette after the vision-
ary of Lourdes and inevitably had been called Bernie since she was an infant. In what her father had
called a conflict in vocations, she liked tennis and
golf equally, but in the end she chose golf, because
of the scholarship, which made it seem a smart decision. It was not. St. Clare's was a prosperous
Franciscan college for women, but it was located in
Wisconsin where the weather reduced the golf season almost to summer itself, a hardship for a college
team. Their matches were usually played in the
Southwest and South against women who had been
golfing nonstop around the calendar. The word
"handicap" was freed from a single use.

On the other hand, she got a fairly good education and she met Augie O'Brien, the golf coach. He
was three years older and had taken the job to tide
him over until he qualified as a touring pro. They
married a week after she graduated. Augie took a job
as assistant teaching pro at the Meadowbrook
Country Club, one of the courses that had sprung up
west of Chicago to accommodate the new housing

developments. Bernie worked in the pro shop and gave a few lessons herself.

"It's nice," her mother said, when she first saw the quarters the senior pro had turned over to them when he bought a condo. "Do you have to pay rent?"

"Of course."

Her mother, not a spare pound on her, hair gray in a way that had the effect of making her seem a younger woman trying to look older, said, "Well, it's convenient."

It was an extension of the pro shop, which is why they got it. The head pro said he wanted to be off duty when he was off duty. She and Augie loved it, waking to the twittering of birds, looking out on fairways glistening with dew in the first rays of the sun, able to play six, sometimes even nine holes together before the first players arrived.

Of course her mother was thinking of later, of how they would live permanently. Bernie had some notion of this point of view. She had the nesting instinct, after all she was a Doyle, but for now, for who knew how long, *this* was what she and Augie wanted, and they wanted to enjoy it without the hint that they were postponing real life, mistaking a game for work, and all the other unstated contrasts her mother's patience conveyed to her.

Neither one of her parents golfed. When she told Augie this, it was with apprehension. Even at St.

Clare's, members of the golf team were second- and third-generation golfers. What would Augie think of her, the equivalent of a wetback?

"Neither were mine. My dad ran the grounds crew and I caddied, played every chance I got, and the rest—" he smiled ruefully "—is history."

One of her jobs, Bernie saw early on, was to make sure he didn't lose confidence in himself. In her heart of hearts, she knew he would never become a touring pro. He was good, very good, but so were the thousands of others who could not survive the intensity of competitive pressure. Shots made with ease in practice were unmakable when large sums of money rode on them and a gallery pressed in, making concentration hard. Augie went up the ladder in the Open several times, but it always ended with a missed putt he could have made with his eyes closed any other time or a scuffed shot from off the fringe, the kind he would deliberately make in giving lessons by way of a warning.

So far as golf went, the pro shop at Meadowbrook, or a course very much like it, was their likely future. A very nice life, but then she had always thought the life her mom and dad had was a nice life. Nonetheless, Bernie sensed that what her mother was saying was, Do you want to end up like me?

Augie's parents were divorced, which made it awkward at the wedding when both of them came.

His father, whom he hadn't seen for something like five years, was a head taller than Augie, bald, with a magnificent face, the eyes pouched and sadly wise, the nose noble, a great square chin, and a mouth that seemed slightly open even when it was closed. His Thai wife came to his elbow. They made an exotic couple. Augie's mother had not remarried, but her consciousness had been raised and she came with several tough-looking female friends who frowned through the marriage ceremony as if they were witnessing a doomed primitive rite.

"Was Augie raised Catholic?"

"He's as good a Catholic as I am.'

Her father intervened. "We talked. He's a good boy, and he understands what getting married means."

Her mother made a little noise. "I wonder if anyone ever does."

When did she first have the feeling that she was more grown up than her mother? A little discontent can be a good thing, but her mother lived in the apparent conviction that she had been cheated out of her patrimony by matrimony. Was living with Gregory Doyle, raising three children with their three birthdays every year, seeming to make her age three times as fast, a death sentence? To be somewhere else, doing something else, to be someone else—her mother was like a teenager at a pajama party who didn't like her hair or name or legs.

She took a quick course at Loyola and, when the space next to the bookstore became available, started a travel agency. It only made things worse. Arranging great trips for other people was not what she wanted.

"Greg, there's this terrific off-season bargain, ten days in Hong Kong, airfare and hotel, double occupancy, for only—"

"Hong Kong!"

"The city, not the gorilla. Greg, let's go."

They went to Hong Kong. But soon there were package deals to Pago Pago, a dream week in Paris, a theater binge in London.

"Let's take a suite in the Palmer House for the weekend and explore Chicago."

"Chicago!"

Brian and Tom thought she was just going through a stage. She was a little kooky now because she had no one to worry about. Bernie knew better. Her mother's wanderlust was the blossoming of something that had always been there.

Her mother had also taken correspondence courses in writing, dreaming of becoming a notorious novelist. She got bogged down in Lesson Three. She looked into the requirements for a teaching certificate, in the grip of the notion that she would go into an inner-city school, transform it, and be the subject of a TV program. It would have taken forever. It didn't matter; her mother had already lived that life in her imagination and was ready for another. A history professor she'd had in college, Sister Mary Teresa something, urged her to think big, not to undervalue herself, to dream dreams. It turned out that she was still consulting the nun.

"She's still alive!"

Her mother took that as a reference to her age rather than the nun's, and Bernie supposed in a way it was. Was this nun encouraging her mother to keep her options open and go on dreaming of what she would do when she grew up?

It was painful to witness the strain between her parents. The boys were partly right. Before they had grown up and left the house, their mother had distractions from her discontent, but now she had all day to wish life were different from what it was. The boys sided with her, urging Dad to take the old girl on another trip. Bernie of course took her father's side. He had provided a good home for his wife and children; he was doing well in a very competitive business, one that required surprising amounts of lore. She had no idea where he had picked it all up. It turned out he dealt with Sister Mary Teresa too.

"Tell her to quit encouraging Mom to think she is just starting out in life."

Her dad's mustache lifted to reveal his teeth. "If you knew her, you'd know she isn't doing that."

"Mom always invokes her authority."

"Well, the devil can quote scripture."

Figure that one out. He always gave her credit for more perception than she had. He had always supported her when he saw she was really intent on something—golf rather than tennis, St. Clare's rather than a probationary scholarship elsewhere, marrying Augie.

A year ago her mother had telephoned and said in a high false voice that she had left her father and was in Milwaukee trying to think things through.

"Milwaukee!"

"It's in Wisconsin."

"Mother, don't be funny. You aren't serious. You've been married forever."

"It does seem that way."

"Oh, cut it out. You're acting about thirteen years old—"

Her mother had hung up. Bernie called Milwaukee hotels, but there was no Margaret Doyle registered. And then the thought came. The first hotel she called back had a Margaret Nelson registered.

"Mother? Don't you dare hang up on me again."

"I've been waiting for you to call."

"Have you? Do you know how difficult it was to find you, Margaret Nelson?"

"Bernie, if you're going to take that tone, there's no point talking. I have thought of doing what I have done longer than I can tell you. It's not as if I were deserting my children. It's not as if your father will really miss me. I just thank God I have some years left for myself."

"What are your plans?"

"Bernie, for now I just wanted to let you know. Will you tell the boys?"

"You want me to tell them you're leaving Dad?"

"They'll understand."

In that she was right, or nearly so. Brian developed a theory. People live longer than they used to, they're not all used up by marrying and having kids. What's to keep them together after they've done the job they got together to do?

"Love?"

"At their age? Come on."

Bernie thought the harsh reality of living alone would bring her mother to her senses. She didn't stay in Milwaukee, of course. She came back to her travel bureau, so she saw her husband every day. The divorce went through smoothly. Whatever he had was half hers, whatever she had was hers. She got the house; her father bought a condo on the North Shore. Bernie watched it all happening and never really believed it. Until her mother told her she was marrying again.

"Please don't get going about it, Bernie. There's nothing to discuss. I'll want you and the boys to come."

"Oh, Mother. Just run away and do it in Las Vegas or some such place."

"It's Philip's idea."

"Who is Philip?"

"We met on a cruise."

"I saw the movie. Will you wear white?"

"If you want me to hang up on you I will."

"I'm coming over."

Bernie hung up. It was just after 7 A.M. Augie was playing an instructional round with a member. She left a note, got into the car, and was shortly caught up in the nightmare of morning traffic. It was after eight when she got to the house in which she'd been raised. The kitchen door was unlocked—they had never locked it—and she stepped inside, calling out.

"Mom, it's me."

The place, that message, made her feel about nine years old again. She went right on upstairs and into her mother's room. The place was a mess. And then she saw the body.

THREE

"DON'T ASK," Geoffrey Stone invariably said when asked where he taught. He was ashamed of the school, and those he eventually told were appalled that a man of his accomplishments and learning was teaching *there.*

The truth was, he was happy enough. Had he ever been really happy? Had anyone? He had taught at more prestigious places and thought his colleagues were kidding when they professed not to know or care what he was working on. His present colleagues were Socratically wise. They knew nothing and knew it. He'd gotten offers, from places like Wyoming and Mississippi, towns he'd never heard of. He wasn't interested. He was a Midwesterner and a city boy, and while he would have slashed his wrists in graduate school if he had known he would end up where he was, he was reconciled to it.

He had tons of time for his own work; he could put in three days at the Newberry Library every week, where he was now in the process of arranging a lecture series. Because of that, today he would have lunch in a convent as the guest of Sister Mary Teresa Dempsey. Getting her for his series had been a real coup. He had read everything she had written and had actually thought she was dead, because the periodical literature stopped a few years back.

"She is writing a book," one of the assistants at the Newberry told him. "Her chef d'oeuvre."

He got her on the phone, explained what he had in mind, said he realized how busy she was, but as one who had read her every word he knew what a contribution she could make. She invited him to lunch.

"No, let me take you."

"I never dine in public places except in an emergency. I think you'll agree this is not an emergency."

What do you call being invited to lunch at a convent?

He was a little taken aback when he knocked at the door of the house on Walton Street and it was answered by a pretty young redhead.

"I must have the wrong house." He stepped back and looked nearsightedly for the number.

"Professor Stone?"

"Is this where I'll find Dr. Dempsey?"

"Come in, come in."

The next fifteen minutes were spent in a tour of the house, a beautiful example of Wright at his strongest.

"Far better than that at the University of Chicago."

"We are particularly grateful for it," the old nun told him. Looking at the house was a distraction from staring at her outfit. He was reminded of women in Flanders wearing native costume for the tourist trade. Was this the author of the stuff he so much admired? "It is our refuge in a time of adversity."

She saved the study until last. How could any scholar sit in such a room, at least on a first visit? He browsed along the shelves, to the obvious approval of his hostess.

"Muratori! Your own?"

"Oh, there's a story to that set. But then there's a story to most old books, isn't there?"

Geoffrey Stone was half through lunch before it occurred to him again that he had been apprehensive about this visit. By then he knew he could tell Sister Mary Teresa how he felt.

"Professor, there are Catholics, perhaps a majority now, who would find this habit as strange as you do."

He looked quizzically at the redhead, who wore a blouse and skirt yet was called Sister by the old nun.

"Are you a novice, Sister?"

"Why would you think that?"

"Well, the way you're dressed."

A great burst of laughter from the old nun, and he soon realized he had walked into one of her pet theories. He gathered she had lost the battle in the order to retain the traditional habit or to modify it so slightly it would be recognizably the same. Her opponents had argued that it would remove the barrier between religious and laity.

"Hasn't it, though? You would not have recognized that Sister Kimberly is a nun."

"I wear a veil when I go out," the redhead said, not at all put out at being the object of such teasing.

"How many others wear the habit?"

"Professor Stone, we three are the remnant of the order."

He actually felt sad, he who would have thought nuns were a carryover from the Dark Ages if he thought of them at all, which he didn't.

"I gather you're not Catholic, Professor Stone?" Sister Kimberly asked.

"No." Both of them waited. "I'm nothing."

"Well, you were created from nothing anyway," the old nun said and went briskly on. "Let's talk about your lecture series."

He told her that anything she wished to talk on having to do with twelfth-century intellectual history would be most welcome. Her book, he had been told, was an intellectual history of the twelfth century.

"Fine, fine. The principle of organization of my work is the rivers of Europe. Ah, you are surprised.

In intellectual history we have perhaps overlooked the role of commerce in the spread of a civilization that could sustain learning. The rivers were nature's highways, of course; we see as a global phenomenon that any city with a history is built upon a river or on some body of water. I propose to give a sketch of the Rhône Valley—Lyon, Avignon, Arles—in the second half of the twelfth century. Would that interest you?''

''The Jews of Avignon are a special interest of mine.''

''During the Avignon papacy?''

''Of course.''

''Then I trust you will note how well treated Jews were by those popes.''

''That's much later than your interests.''

It was, but long ago, when she was a young religious, she had accompanied her superior to Rome to see some cardinal in charge of religious orders, and as a reward they had taken a side trip to Avignon.

''I feel about it as Saint Chattering of Siena did. Now it is a ghost town—so far as the papacy goes, I mean. I spent two lovely days in the archives there.''

Geoffrey was surprised that it was already one-thirty when they rose from the table. Sister Mary Teresa as he now thought of her—Dr. Dempsey did not begin to suggest her personality—had been more of a treat than he had expected. She came with him to the door, making use of a cane.

"You must tell me sometime the story of your Muratori."

"I will give you a clue. Do you by any chance know Gregory Doyle?"

"I know his shop, of course. I don't think I've seen things there nearly as valuable as some of the things in your study."

On his way up the street to his car, Stone decided he would detour by the Newberry and let it be known that he had brought off his coup.

FOUR

THROUGHOUT LUNCH Kim marveled at the way Emtee Dempsey had seemingly put out of her mind the dreadful news about Margaret Nelson Doyle. Even when the old nun mentioned the dead woman's former husband, the book dealer, there was no indication at all that tragedy had struck the Doyle family that morning. Before Professor Stone's arrival, the old nun had made clear she wanted Kim to get in contact as quickly as possible with the Doyle family. That had proved impossible before lunch.

"Immediately afterward then, if you would, Sister. What did Katherine have to say?"

"She hadn't heard the news before I called. She's working at home today, or at least she intended to."

Even as they spoke the front doorbell rang, and a moment later they could hear Katherine Senski's hearty voice greeting Joyce.

"Ah, still up. I thought you'd all be down for your afternoon naps."

She was grinning when she looked into the study.

"I hope you didn't hear me."

"Katherine, is that you? You enter with all the fe-line footwork of Sandburg's fog. How would one know you're in the house?"

"I was jogging in the neighborhood and thought I'd stop by." Katherine was unwilling to be topped by her old friend.

Kim laughed aloud at the image of the septuage-narian Katherine jogging up Walton Street. Her costumes ran to the elaborate and dramatic, dresses that on her seemed to be introducing a new style rather than recalling an old one. "Sister Joyce can lend you one of her jogging costumes."

"Enough, enough!" cried Sister Mary Teresa. "Tell me what you know of Margaret Doyle's death."

Katherine had worked as a reporter and colum-nist at the *Tribune* so long she remembered Colonel Robert McCormick, its legendary Anglophobe pub-lisher. His prejudice extended to the language itself, or so his introduction of "rationalized spelling" into the pages of the *Tribune* could have been inter-preted. Thank God, that had not outlived him. Em-tee Dempsey predicted a similar short life for "inclusive language."

Katherine had talked with the reporters who had been on the scene. "You can read what survives ed-iting in the evening edition. But this is what they learned."

The nude untoweled body of Margaret had been found where she had fallen when struck on the back of the head, apparently as she came out of the bathroom to investigate the noise the intruder must have made tearing the room apart. The water in the shower was still running when the daughter found her mother. There had been no sexual attack, only the lethal blow that killed her. Her purse was on the table beside the bed; in it was a thousand dollars' worth of traveler's checks and an array of credit cards. Nothing seemed to be taken. Despite the mayhem created by the intruder, there was no indication of what he was after.

"Or whether he had found it?"

"Or whether he had found it. He did go on looking after he killed Margaret, however."

"How is that known?"

"The murder instrument was a marble replica of Michelangelo's David, about a foot high, the kind so many tourists bring back from Florence. It was found on the dresser, and items in the bottom dresser drawer seem to have been used to wipe bloodstains from his hands."

"You keep saying he and him and his."

"There is a partial footprint in some spilled talcum. A man's shoe."

"A thief who did not steal and who apparently killed without premeditation?"

Katherine nodded. "The police will of course be speaking to Gregory Doyle. Do you think him capable of such a deed?"

Emtee Dempsey's eyes rounded. "I think anyone capable of any deed in certain circumstances. It will be discovered that he was much provoked by his wife."

"The intruder let himself in by the back door and went immediately upstairs; grass cuttings from the recently mowed lawn enabled them to track his entry. The reporter—it's young Cousins, by the way; you met her, Sister Kimberly—heard the police say that the man knew his way around."

"Who's in charge?"

Katherine looked at Kim. "Richard."

Emtee Dempsey beamed, as if having Kim's brother on the case gave them special entrée. The reverse would be more like it; Emtee Dempsey should rely on Katherine. Nonetheless she asked Kim to ask her brother whether Gregory Doyle was a suspect.

"Whatever he says," Katherine said, "the answer will be yes."

"Poor foolish Margaret." Emtee Dempsey sighed. During the morning, they had gone to their chapel and recited the Sorrowful Mysteries of the rosary for the repose of her soul. "She spent her whole life thinking she had boarded the wrong train. Have you seen this?"

She handed over the wedding invitation that had come that morning. Katherine gasped when she read it. "May I use your phone?"

Without waiting for permission, she dialed, asked for Laura Cousins, and proceeded to read the legend on the wedding invitation.

"I thought you might not have known. That means the police may not either. I would lead off with this if I were you."

Katherine hung up, glanced at the invitation again, then put it on Emtee Dempsey's desk. "Methodist?"

"Well, she could hardly stage a formal wedding in a Catholic church. Presumably Mr. Philip Chesney Cord is a Methodist."

"Who is he?"

"I was about to ask you the same question."

Kim went into the kitchen to try again to reach Bernadette O'Brien, the daughter who had discovered her mother's body. This time she succeeded.

"Mrs. O'Brien, you don't know me, but I'm calling for Sister Mary Teresa Dempsey, who taught your mother years ago."

"I know."

"Your mother mentioned her?"

"Ad nauseam. What do you want?"

What had seemed an opening door had been slammed shut in her face. But Kim persisted, asking if there was any possibility that she might talk with her.

"About what?"

"Sister Mary Teresa takes a special interest in her former students. She received a wedding invitation this morning—"

"What?"

"You knew of this, of course."

"What did you say your name is?"

"Kimberly Moriarity. I work for Sister Mary Teresa. She is, as you can imagine, quite an elderly woman now. Could you give me a few minutes of your time? It will mean an awful lot to Sister and—"

"Why don't you talk to my father?"

"Sister hopes to talk with him herself."

"And you're stuck with me."

"Could I come now?"

"Oh, why not."

When she was given the address of a golf club, Kim was surprised. A round of golf after what Bernadette had learned did not seem likely.

"My husband's assistant pro, in case you're wondering."

"Thanks. I was."

After she hung up, Joyce said, "Did you say Meadowbrook?"

"Her husband works there."

"They're bidding for the Western Open. That must be some course."

"Want to come along?"

Joyce clearly would have loved to, but she shook her head. The house might seem informal, but both she and Joyce owed religious obedience to Sister Mary Teresa, who was their superior. They did not come and go at their own whim. Besides, Joyce had her own tasks for the afternoon.

"What's her husband's name?"

"O'Brien.'

"Augie O'Brien?"

"Is he somebody?"

"He nearly made the Open last year."

Kim did not ask Joyce what that meant. Joyce's interest in sports was keen; she avidly read *The Sporting News* and *Sports Illustrated,* to which she subscribed with Sister Mary Teresa's approval. The old nun respected detailed knowledge in any form, and Joyce was a talking data bank. She really would be good to have along. Kim went into the study and suggested this, but Emtee Dempsey shook her head.

"I feel a little guilty sending you, Sister. I don't think you'll learn much."

"Then why bother?"

"That's a reasonable question. My answer is that you will learn something. I expect far more of Gregory. Mr. Rush made inquiries, and Gregory has seen the wisdom of being represented by someone from Mr. Rush's firm. The two of them will drop by this evening.''

FIVE

As a boy Gregory Doyle had attended St. Bede's, a boarding school run by Benedictine monks in southern Wisconsin, equidistant between Madison and Milwaukee, and for a time he had even thought he had a vocation to the monastic life. He had been fascinated when he learned of the role monasteries had played during the Dark Ages, keeping learning alive, monks copying manuscripts in the scriptorium, trading them with other communities, building up a library. Whenever he found himself becoming used to books, he would think of the thousands of years before printing when texts were written out a letter at a time on parchment or animal skin. Imagine making your own copy of a book. Not a photocopy, a handwritten copy. Even using a medieval shorthand, making your own copy of the Bible, say, would have been an enormous undertaking. If you had the skins, if you had the parchment, if you had the time. He learned to cherish books.

The love of books stayed with him. He began collecting at an early age, and his hobby developed into his career. He bought and sold private libraries, he searched for titles that were rare to the point of nonexistence, and he dealt with manuscripts. His little hoard of these was kept in the vault of his store. He spent time at Praglia, a monastery near Padua, where he learned the skills of preservation, restoration, and binding. The asking value of his personal collection made him a wealthy man. He had done well.

The great cross of his life had been his wife's lack of enthusiasm for his work. Margaret regarded what he did for a living as something that should have remained a hobby. There were some lines lettered on a scrap of the paper Doyle made, a motto of one of Kierkegaard's books, Shakespeare translated back into English from the German version. "Better well hung than ill wed." A sardonic thought, and one into which he could not fully enter. He loved Margaret.

Despite her discontents, in part because of them, she had been an adventure to live with. She had talents that could have been used in many ways, but for years she had devoted herself heart and soul to raising the kids. Not without complaining, of course, but the fact that she realized there were alternatives made what she was doing all the more impressive.

He had been really disappointed when she decided to open a travel agency. There are two kinds of traveler, business and tourist. The former knows why he is going somewhere and wants to get there as swiftly and cheaply as he can. The latter seemed to inspire in Margaret a vague wanderlust and a sense that life had passed her by.

Their estrangement seemed to have begun in the first years of their marriage. The separation she asked for after the children were gone and she'd had some success with her travel bureau was both devastating and somehow expected. When did he first realize that Margaret had not given him the whole of her life? But the divorce!

"Margaret, what's the point? How much freer could you be?"

"That *is* the point. Why pretend something still exists when it doesn't?"

"Because of the children."

"Greg." She turned her head slightly and looked at him. "They're as acquainted with your egoism as I am."

His dedication to his business and his efforts to succeed and, in succeeding, to do something worthwhile were appreciated by the kids, he hoped, but he knew Margaret thought the kids saw her as the injured party. In the case of the boys, she was probably right.

"You should humor her more, Dad."

"I suppose you're right."

"You can take more time off now. Why not travel?"

"Travel is broadening," he agreed. His irony went unnoticed by Tom and was one of Margaret's legitimate gripes against him. Bernie was too much on his side.

"Take the first step yourself. If she doesn't want to live under your roof, she has abandoned you."

"She has the house, Bernie."

"Why did you let her have it? That makes it look as if she's the injured party. She is the most selfish person I have ever known."

"Bernie, she's your mother."

"I didn't say I didn't love her."

Brian actually threatened their father for moving out of the house. "What a rotten thing to do to her. You know how she is about what people think. That whole neighborhood has got to be buzzing."

"Talk to her for me."

"Dad, step one is getting over your pride and going back to her."

It was a lesson on the way the same events meant totally different things to well-informed observers. Gregory Doyle did not consider himself an Evelyn Waugh hero, doomed to be treated like dirt by his spouse and, all innocent, taking it with a stiff upper lip. Joking about their troubles met with little success. His suggestion when he moved out that they share the services of Lavinia the cleaning lady was solemnly agreed to by Margaret. Odd how Lavinia seemed a line back into his past life. Whenever Margaret had gotten started ticking off his faults and deficiencies, he could have added to the list. He would have removed some items too, of course; he was damned if he would think of his status as an antiquarian book dealer as anything but an accomplishment.

He had started college in a naval program during the war, V-5, aimed at producing pilots. But the war ended before he ever saw an airplane; he had finished the remaining semesters on the GI Bill and had a degree from a school he would never have chosen in the free market. Nor would he have taken an engineering degree in other circumstances. But his mind had been formed at St. Bede's; he had become acquainted with the head librarian at his college and was delighted to find so intelligent a man on so obscure a campus. It was then he began to see the possibilities of a career and not just a hobby in books.

When Margaret's father, a lawyer, spent their first meeting making obscure references to accounting, Greg was puzzled. Margaret, it turned out, had told her father that her fiancé was a bookkeeper.

"I couldn't just tell him you buy and sell books. It sounds like a garage sale."

"Your father has an interesting collection."

But he had diverted Greg's questions back to the intricacies of double entry bookkeeping, a gentleman who wanted to put his prospective son-in-law at ease. Perhaps Gregory Doyle should have seen the significance of that misdescription of what he did, but at the time he had thought it a hilarious joke.

He was reminded of the divorce now when it was suggested that someone from Benjamin Rush's firm would represent him.

"Represent me?"

It was his first realization that he had not only lost Margaret but he would also become a suspect in her death.

Rush was an elderly distinguished man who seemed to know who Gregory was. He spoke with great deference and indirection.

"Sister Mary Teresa Dempsey suggested I look in on you and see how you're being treated."

"An old friend of my wife's," Greg mused. "And of mine. I suppose I should more properly call her a customer."

"She spoke of you as a friend."

"That's kind of her."

"I am sorry to be talking to you at so sad a time. What a shock this must have been for you."

"It was more shocking to hear the news from our daughter."

Rush seemed more at ease now, as if a ritual dance was just what the occasion called for. An allusion having been made to the reason for the visit and somewhat equivocal condolences expressed, a few remarks about books were in order. He mentioned his lifelong devotion to William Dean Howells. Rush would certainly not be among those who criticized Howells for lack of explicitness in his treatment of relations between men and women. Gregory was almost surprised when Rush cited *Indian Summer* as Howells's best.

"I am sure you have thought of what faces you now, Mr. Doyle."

"Not really."

"I will not myself handle the case, though I assure you I will keep a close eye on it. I suggest Irene Maloney. She is young, but—"

"I know her. She is a friend of my daughter's."

"Very well. There are of course others."

"I wasn't objecting. Irene will be just fine."

"Sometimes in such matters it is best not to have friends involved."

"Like Sister Mary Teresa?"

"Touché. Very well. Miss Maloney will be in touch with you. And let us hope we are making provisions for something that will never arise."

SIX

BERNIE WAS IN the pro shop when the battered little
VW came chugging up the drive, its motor so loud it
should have been doing sixty rather than the falter-
ing twenty it was making on the moderate upslope
from the county road. At the counter, two women—
who if the best and latest in equipment made good
golfers would be in the Hall of Fame—looked out at
the VW, then at one another, then at Bernie.

"Someone has made a wrong turn," Mrs. Waddles said.

"I hope so," Mrs. Wiggles replied.

"I'll go see. Got everything you need?"

"You must show me this sometime," Mrs. Wiggles said, frowning at the all-purpose fairway wood
Augie had on display. Gimmicks are surefire with
uncertain golfers. Boris, pushing a broom, might
have been trying to sweep the ladies off their feet.
Proletarian resentment gleamed in Boris's eye when
he glared at these overweight women chattering
about golf clubs. Bernie half wished he would ha-
rangue them with his radical views. Why had Boris
of all people ended up working at a country club?

"Later," Sasha promised and went outside to intercept the VW.

The redhead at the wheel definitely wasn't a member, and the only place for clubs in that car would be in the empty back seat.

"Can I help you?"

"Are you Bernadette O'Brien?"

They were both yelling in order to be heard over the VW's motor. Bernie nodded and looked more closely at the driver.

"Where can I put this?"

"That's a pretty leading question."

"What?"

Bernie got in front of the VW and waved her into the pro's parking space. Suddenly she was sure who the redhead was.

"What a lovely view," Sister Kimberly said a moment later when they sat on the terrace with the eighteenth green just beneath them and the course in all its verdant glory spread out before them. "And you're here every day?"

There was no way that anyone was going to think of being a golf professional as a job. She and Augie had simply stopped trying, smiling at the implication that they were playing their lives away and being paid for it besides. Today Bernie was waiting for unexpressed disapproval that she should be here after what had happened to her mother, but so far nothing.

"Are you a nun?" She had to ask.

"Yes."

"Things have changed."

"You can't be old enough to have experienced that."

"Our nuns wore habits." It came out as a kind of accusation.

"We were given the option. Sister Mary Teresa still wears the traditional habit. It is everything people think they want."

She said it without emphasis, but Bernie got the point. She supposed it was with nuns the way it is with nurses; people come into a hospital once in a blue moon to visit a relative and are shocked at what they take to be the callous manner of those who live all day every day with the ill. Nuns are supposed to be super-otherworldly for the worldly.

Kimberly said, "The questions I ask you are really hers. She can't get around as easily as she used to, and not everyone can come to the house to satisfy her curiosity."

"I have to tell you I haven't liked her for a very long time."

"Then you know her?"

"I know of her. My mother talked about her a lot. Sister Mary Teresa encouraged her in ways I suppose were meant well, but they had the effect of strengthening my mother's weaknesses.''

"What weaknesses?"

Bernie inhaled slowly and looked down to where Wiggles and Waddles were preparing to tee off on the first hole. "She never grew up. Does anyone completely grow up? I don't know. But my mother had the outlook of a teenager. Nothing was real, everything was possible."

"That's about what Sister Mary Teresa thought. I'm afraid your mother was one of her disappointments."

Bernie reacted by wanting to defend her mother. It was all right if she spoke ill of the dead, but she didn't want anyone else doing it, particularly the woman whose authority her mother had invoked for most of the dumb moves in her life.

"I could make a long list of all the good things she did."

"They divorced?"

"Yeah." Suddenly Bernie wanted to cry. All her mother's nutty dreams about doing great and wonderful things when she only had such a little time to live and she should have spent that time with Dad. She didn't trust herself to speak at the moment, and she felt she was giving the redheaded young nun an advantage.

"Sister Mary Teresa was knocked off her chair when the wedding invitation came."

"What wedding invitation?"

"Your mother's."

"To Dad?" This wasn't making much sense. Sister Kimberly had sat back in her chair, a startled expression on her face.

"Sister received a printed invitation in the mail to your mother's upcoming marriage to someone named..." She closed her eyes for a moment, but her expression was one of confidence she would come up with it. "Cord. Philip Chesney Cord."

Bernie looked at her. She couldn't be joking, not about something like this.

"We assumed you received one too and that is why you went to see her this morning."

Bernie shook her head slowly. Her mother had said what she had in mind, remarrying, but not that she was anywhere near sending out invitations. It had seemed just another fire to put out. And she had forgotten all about it in the aftermath of what she found when she got to the house. She stood. Mrs. Wiggles had just done the main thing they had worked on preventing in her last lesson, swinging as if she were about to throw the hammer in track, ending up struggling to keep her balance, facing the fairway so she got a good view of her ball snap hooking into the woods.

"Let's go check our mail."

"Where is it?"

"It's on the other side of the pro shop." The nun was up and moving in a moment. She had a lithe body and seemed in good shape.

"You ever golf?"

"Just a little tennis."

Maybe she should ask her to come out and play. You were supposed to do nice things for nuns, so they would pray for you. Had they prayed for Mom? Again she felt tears near. They ran into Augie as they passed the pro shop.

"Giving a lesson?"

"Augie, this is Kimberly. Sister Kimberly." She tried not to lower her voice but she did. "Were you home just now?"

"Yeah, why?"

"Had the mail come?"

"Did it ever. There are three magazine subscription companies that want to make you a millionaire and an armful of the slickest mail-order catalogs you ever saw."

"First class mail?"

"What am I telling you about?"

She threw a playful punch and he danced out of range. More or less consciously they played the cutesy couple. She and Kim went on to the house, but there was no wedding invitation. Bernie got on the phone to her brothers, who were coming for Margaret's funeral.

"Thinking of making it legal?" Brian responded when she asked if he had received a wedding invitation.

"I guess that means you didn't."

"Who's getting married?"

"When will you be getting in?"

"I leave here at two, touch down at O'Hare in time to hit the traffic. Do I go to the house?"

"You better not. It's off limits for now."

"I suppose it would be. Bernie, I still can't believe this happened. You got room for me?"

"We'll make room. Shall I pick you up?"

"Are you picking up Tom?"

"He didn't ask."

"I'll take a cab. It sounds awful in the circumstances, but should I bring my clubs?"

"To a golf course? If you don't we'll lend you a beginner's set."

Tom hadn't received the wedding invitation either. He couldn't talk, he was wrapping up a few things before he left, and she let him go.

"Dad didn't mention it," she said to Kim. "Would she send one to him? I'm afraid she would. To show it was really all right and he better not think otherwise. Oh, I wish I could stop saying things about her. I loved her."

She did cry now, in the privacy of her own home, with only a nun who didn't look like a nun as witness. When she got control of herself, she put on coffee and they sat in the kitchen. Kimberly loved everything about their place.

"Everyone does." She stopped herself from mentioning her mother's reaction. "So what are the questions you were supposed to ask me?"

"Look, we don't have to if you'd rather not. I can find out most of it from the police."

"Like what?"

"The layout of the house, exactly what happened when you came in, where the body was. But she would want to see it with your eyes."

"What in the world for?"

"You sound like my brother Richard."

Richard Moriarity? Yes, there was a resemblance, over and above the red hair.

"Is she an amateur detective or what?"

"Anything that concerns women who were students of hers she takes to be her business. She just doesn't have it in her to sit around and see how the police will explain how your mother was killed. She thinks she can do as good a job and more quickly. And she's usually right."

"I think I would like to meet her."

"I know she's going to ask you to come talk with her at Walton Street. It's where our house is."

"Your convent?"

"Yes. It's no clubhouse, but you'll like it."

"Did my mom go there?"

"Not as often as she should have."

SEVEN

"COULD I SEE that invitation again?" Katherine Senski asked. Joyce had brought her a glass of wine, and the four of them were settled down on the sun porch at Walton Street. "At the moment a little corroboration would ease my mind."

Katherine had just come from an emergency meeting at the paper. Lawyers for Philip Chesney Cord had contacted the paper's lawyers to protest the suggestion in the story about the death of Margaret Nelson Doyle that a wedding was planned between the two of them. They wondered how soon they could expect to see a prominent correction of this disinformation. Wilson the editor looked at Laura Cousins the reporter who looked to Katherine the source.

"I saw the invitation myself," Katherine had told them.

"Good. Our lawyers would appreciate getting a look at it."

"If one has been received, dozens of others will have been received."

"Then why is Cord making a stink about it?"

"They called it disinformation?"

Wilson fumbled through some papers on his desk, found what he wanted, and brought it within inches of his eyes. "Disinformation."

"That's what they said as well as what you wrote down?"

"Who's on the carpet here anyway, you and Laura or me? You'll remember that, on your advice, Laura swung the story around the wedding invitation. A great idea. I loved it. But the man's lawyers call it disinformation. Should I spell it?"

"It's an odd choice of word. Disinformation is an effort to mask what you're really doing by telling lies."

"Then let me interpret. The mask we wear is of a paper that gives its readers the truth the better to tell them lies." Wilson didn't like it himself. "Maybe they don't use the word as you do."

"It is not a matter of how I use the word. It is a matter of what the word means. I expect lawyers to be precise in what they say. It is libelous to suggest that we deliberately printed a falsehood in order to pursue some other goal."

"Maybe you should be there when our lawyers meet his."

"I would like to be. In fact, I insist on it." Throughout, Katherine was conscious she was playing to an audience that was not there; namely, her friend on Walton Street.

She took a cab from the paper to Walton Street and still aquiver with righteous anger told Joyce imperiously that she would like a glass of wine, please, she had things to say. Kim brought the invitation to Emtee Dempsey and she studied it closely, then passed it on to Katherine. Katherine would never have admitted the relief she felt when once more her eyes read the legend.

"What is Philip Chesney Cord's game?" Katherine demanded.

"Not wanting his name in a story telling of the murder of someone is understandable enough," Emtee Dempsey said, "but this someone was his fiancée; the invitations had gone out. Is the paper often approached by lawyers in this way?"

"Constantly."

By and large, protests arose from the fact that people wished things were otherwise than they were and thought superstitiously that the reporting of an event somehow brought that event about. So even if it had happened, it was the paper's fault.

The old nun made a puffing sound. "Why do lawyers bother with such nonsense?"

"Since Benjamin Rush is not within hearing, I am tempted to answer that," Katherine replied.

"Who is Mr. Cord?"

Katherine smiled. Before she left, she had reassured Laura, counting on the corroboration she had now seen.

"I'm going to find out everything I can about that guy," Laura had said.

"Good. But coolly. He's not our enemy. We're not interested in punishing him. But find out everything you can."

Katherine told Emtee Dempsey this. "Otherwise I would have presumed to bring her along. You three would love her. All she drinks is Diet Pepsi."

"You have no idea who he is?"

"He sails. Isn't that odd? But it's the only thing I thought of when I saw his name on that invitation. It's still the only thing his name suggests."

"Sails."

"Competitively. He's won the Mackinac race twice."

Every summer a regatta from Chicago set off for Mackinac Island in upper Michigan, the race consisting of there and back. Over the years, Katherine had read her share of accounts of the event. Participants came from around the country, Great Lakes sailing presenting its own peculiar challenges, and it was no small matter to place, let alone win.

"Can one make a living sailing?"

"This is all amateur sailing."

Emtee Dempsey gripped the arms of her brocade chair and stared into the fireplace. "I wonder if Margaret even knew him."

"What?"

"Sister Kimberly can tell you that thus far I seem to be the only one who received an invitation. Her children didn't, her husband didn't."

"Former husband," Kim said.

"Husband," Emtee Dempsey repeated.

Katherine finished her wine and made certain Joyce noticed her glass was empty. As she relinquished it, she was feeling less eager to confront Mr. Cord's lawyers. What if there should only be the one invitation? That would generate a kind of speculation which, in lawyers, goes beyond the disagreeable and becomes menacing.

There was that other factor she preferred not to think about. It wasn't that she thought she was immortal or anything like that; she knew that a woman well into her seventies (the way she referred to her age when she could get away with it) is in constant danger of passing a line beyond which the possible patronizing in the manner of the young becomes real and out in the open at last. She had staved it off simply by continuing to be the senior reporter on the *Trib*, doing her share, not resting on her laurels. In that she was like her dear and old friends Sister Mary Teresa and Benjamin Rush. The present situation suddenly held the threat of a crisis that could precipitate all of them into the status of has-beens, slightly gaga, to be spoken to increasingly as children and the ill are spoken to.

Here they were, two old women who in different ways were responsible for the story on Margaret Nelson Doyle's murder being swung around her imminent second marriage. With this contested by the alleged groom, and with no other invitation turning up thus far, it would not take a malevolent mind to think that, perhaps in a silly effort to prove they were still in their prime, they had come upon that invitation by less than straightforward means.

Katherine would never have said it in a million years, but she was in the situation she was in solely because of the invitation Emtee Dempsey had shown her. It was real enough and she had not pretended she wasn't relieved to see it again, but unsettling precedents came to mind when her old friend had engaged in what many would call deception. If she weren't sipping on a second glass of wine after an unsettling day, Katherine would have liked to review everything the old nun had told her about that invitation, to see if perhaps there wasn't smuggled into her remarks the possibility of saying later, "Oh, you thought I said that, did you?" and claim that while she could see why Katherine had mistakenly thought the initiation was an invitation, that is certainly not the meaning she had meant to convey....

Katherine's uneasiness increased, and if, as the Apostle says, a little wine is good for the stomach's sake, more should be even better. She was drawing Joyce's attention to her empty glass when the doorbell rang, and as in a drawing room comedy they all fell silent and looked in the direction of the front door.

EIGHT

KIM GOT UP and went down the hall to answer the bell because she already had a premonition. Sure enough, it was Richard, a preternaturally calm Richard who, without any preliminary outburst or complaint about Sister Mary Teresa's butting into a case he was on, gave her a brotherly kiss and waited to be taken down the hall.

"Is that a new dress?"

"No."

"I thought not. It's becoming a habit."

"Ha-ha. We're in the living room. Would you like something to drink?"

The question was a dead giveaway, but the vertigo she felt was her own and she didn't want him to think he had Sister Mary Teresa at a disadvantage. Kim never offered him anything to drink and objected to the way the old nun had on occasion plied him with alcohol when she was in a tight spot. Kim did not want her brother going the way of certain Moriaritys before them, having trouble with the drink—elbow trouble, her old Aunt Bridget had called it. It was in the family, and a word to the wise is sufficient. Bridget counseled total abstinence but, if not, perpetual vigilance.

"No, thanks," Richard said in response to her question.

This was a very bad omen indeed. When had he ever refused the offer of a drink?

"Ah, the conspiring parties, all gathered together preparing their next step."

"If we had prepared for your coming at this moment, we could not have done better, Richard."

Richard bowed to Emtee Dempsey, took Katherine's large bejeweled hand and brought it to his lips, shook his head at Joyce, and said, "Nothing for me, thanks." He sat down. "But perhaps I should have waited for the invitation." He fixed a now severe eye on the superior of the house.

"Nothing at all, Richard?" Emtee Dempsey sounded as if she were concerned for his health. "That wine isn't entirely bad, is it, Katherine?"

"Wine." As Richard said the word it conjured up hordes of derelicts with their pathetic bottles in paper sacks, huddled against the world, seeking oblivion.

"There is some Jameson's Irish whiskey, a gift of Mr. Rush. I'm told it's the best."

"It's not. But that is not why I've come. I had hoped to speak to you about this as well, Katherine, so it is particularly nice to find you here."

"And what is 'this'?"

He took a photocopy of the *Tribune* story on the slaying of Margaret Nelson Doyle from his pocket. The reduction that made it possible to get it all on a single page necessitated getting out his glasses as well. They were silly-looking little half-lensed glasses that are acceptable on perhaps one out of five who wear them. Richard was not in the happy twenty percent. Besides, she knew he just picked them up in Walgreens for a few dollars: magnifying glasses. He began to read.

"'Margaret Doyle, a Chicago businesswoman whose coming marriage to Philip Chesney Cord had just been announced, was found slain in her lakeshore home. The forty-four-year-old mother of three, founder and operator of a successful travel agency, was discovered by her daughter....' Shall I continue?"

"That is a remarkably effective opening, Katherine," Emtee Dempsey said.

"Laura Cousins is good. Very good."

"Where did she get this stuff about a coming marriage to Cord?"

"From me."

Richard had sat forward, ready for combat, and Katherine's answer disarmed him.

"Where did you get it?"

"That I cannot tell you. Journalistic sources are not divulged, as you know."

"Look, I know Cord's lawyers have talked to the *Trib*. If it comes to that, can you imagine sitting in court and, on a matter like this, invoking your sources?"

"She heard it from me," Emtee Dempsey said.

Kim could see, after a moment of surprise when Sister Mary Teresa volunteered the information he wanted, that Richard was wondering why she would. He looked at Joyce.

"You got any beer?"

"Mr. Rush brought some Guinness stout."

"What is this, St. Patrick's Day?"

"That is when he brought the Jameson's and the Guinness. For our Irish guests."

Richard made it sound like a favor when he accepted Guinness. He turned to Sister Mary Teresa.

"And where would you have heard of a wedding the supposed groom knows nothing about?"

"Did he say that?"

"I just mentioned that his lawyers—"

"Oh, I know about that. But, Richard, you and I know how people like that, sailing people, act under pressure."

"How did you know?"

"Poor Margaret was a former student of mine, and—"

"Not another!"

"Your young colleague might have gotten that into the story too, Katherine. Yes, Richard, the poor woman was an alumna of the college. She kept in touch over the years, as the girls do, and of course I love to keep up on what is happening in their lives."

"And she told you she and Cord were going to marry?"

"Have you yourself talked with him, Richard?"

"He's out of town."

"Since when?"

"I'm not sure. He's in Paris."

"Paris, is it? Well, well. Quite literally flown away. But surely he didn't read about poor Margaret in Paris. Perhaps he read about it before leaving."

"Or perhaps he keeps in contact with Chicago while he's away."

"Look, I don't know why he's in Paris. But that's where he is. The point is—"

"I should think that *is* the point, Richard. Of course I know you're just dissembling, trying to get it off to the side, so you can mislead us into thinking Mr. Cord's absence is not the key to recent events."

Joyce came in with a glass of vile-looking dark ale. Kim had tasted it once and could not imagine why anyone would willingly drink it.

"A flight to Paris from Chicago is going to lose seven or eight hours of clock time. That is, when it's morning here, it's afternoon there. So in order for a flight to arrive at Orly in the early morning, the preferred time, it would leave Chicago... When exactly did Margaret die?''

Kim had seen it happen before, but she marveled at the way the old nun had deflected the question of the invitation and was chattering away with Richard as if she were eager to be of such poor help as she could. Such a performance placed Kim in the unenviable position of rejoicing that the old nun was getting out of a tight spot but regretting that it was her brother who was the victim. Beyond that was the inescapable fact that Emtee Dempsey was not eager to show Richard the wedding invitation and let him make of it what he would.

The old nun would consider it her private mail from an alumna and, if it did turn out to be the only invitation sent—well, that is something she would want to look into herself. It was difficult to think, odd as the possibility of a single invitation's having been sent undoubtedly was, that the one doing it was the person the police were seeking to identify.

''It's the husband she divorced rather than the one you say she hoped to acquire who interests me.''

''Gregory Doyle? The man has the patience of a saint.''

''Maybe he ran out.''

''Why?''

"He says he didn't know about his former wife's plans to remarry."

"Neither did his children."

"Say he did, though."

"Yes."

"What kind of woman was Margaret Doyle?"

For several minutes her listeners would have been pardoned if they thought Sister Mary Teresa was proposing Margaret for canonization. She had been a good wife and mother; her children were—do you remember the words of the Roman matron?—*margaritae suae?*

"No, but I'll have another Guinness."

"Her jewels," Emtee Dempsey translated.

She nodded at Joyce to serve their guest another stout.

"She kept in touch, and we talked about her life. Hers is a not unusual case of a sensible woman having her consciousness raised, as it is unfortunately called. She read silly things, listened to sillier women, and became discontented with her lot in life. Discontent had been the source of virtue before, prodding her always to do better what she was doing. It became the source of her undoing. She began to think there was some life elsewhere more fulfilling than the one in which she was engaged."

"She divorced him."

"They separated. I think Gregory thought that would suffice. *I* thought it would suffice. Margaret may have lost some illusions, but she became stubborn. She did not want to admit that she was chasing a rainbow."

"So she divorced him."

"Yes. He put no obstacles in her way when he saw she was serious. She got far more than she asked: the house, her car. Gregory was the one who was thrown into the world, so to speak."

"Did he resent it?"

"I am sure he grieved over the crumbling of his marriage. But fortunately he had his work."

"Selling books."

"That does not quite capture what he does, Richard."

"Capture it for me."

She took him into the study and drew his attention to certain books there, books Gregory Doyle had found for her. "Most dealers would simply say such titles are not to be found. And they would be right. They are not found, they are discovered. Gregory has the knack of discovery. He is also adept in the restoration of books, both printed and manuscript. His own collection would be the envy of many."

"Collectibles?"

"Richard, you do have a way of diminishing things."

"I'm trying to settle who killed the man's wife. So far he looks like the one. Where was he during the previous day, Sunday? He spent all day at his shop. Did anyone know he was there? Lavinia, the cleaning lady, vouches for it, but of course she wasn't there. He doesn't open on Sunday, that's why it's such a good day to work. Does he still have keys to the house on the North Shore? Yes. Whoever entered the house knew it well, knew precisely where he was going."

"Circumstantial."

"Now who's diminishing things?"

"Richard, I think you are barking up the wrong tree."

"So what's the right tree?"

"I haven't the faintest idea."

Richard watched her closely as she spoke. "Straight, no baloney, no mental reservations?"

"I haven't the faintest idea who killed Margaret Nelson Doyle."

Kim heard this admission almost with relief, until the old nun added, "But I am as determined as you are to find out."

NINE

IRENE MALONEY HAD BEEN second in her class at the Notre Dame Law School; she had been a fellow of the White Center, on the board of the law journal, and in her last semester taught an undergraduate course in the philosophy of law for the Department of Philosophy. Her destiny seemed to be an academic career, that possibility came up in almost every extended conversation she had with her professors, and at the time she could feel the attraction of returning to the campus after some years of practice. Now she doubted that she ever would, or could. Her forte now seemed to be the courtroom. She was not surprised when Ben Rush approached her about the murder of Margaret Doyle.

"There has been no overt accusation, let alone an arraignment, but he needs counsel now."

Irene was almost disappointed. The prospect of defending a man accused of murder attracted her. Obviously Doyle had not asked for her.

"Do you know him, Mr. Rush?"

"No, but a friend of mine asked me to look into it. I have and I found him to be a very plausible man, a book dealer, very knowledgeable in his field but I suspect naive in matters of the law. I have told him to stop talking until you and I had a little discussion."

"You think he's innocent?"

His snow-white mustache twitched slightly. If she were ever to fall in love with a man in his seventies, it would be Ben Rush. It was he who interviewed her, and when he said, "Ah, Notre Dame," she'd said she didn't know a thing about the football team.

"Do they have a team?"

It was her first encounter with his straight-faced irony and she had nearly explained to him that, yes, the University of Notre Dame has a football team of some reputation.

"Of course I think he's innocent." He paused. "But then I think everyone is innocent, sometimes even after they have been tried and convicted."

Meaning, Go and talk with the man and start from scratch. "Who is your friend?"

He smiled. "Someone I have known for many years. Why do you ask?"

"I want to know if I have a rival."

He actually blushed. "Her name is Sister Mary Teresa Dempsey, and she is seventy-seven years old."

"The dangerous age."

"I shall take you to see her sometime."

Before talking to her putative client, she went to the detective division, where she was directed to Inspector Richard Moriarity, a rangy redhead with a crooked smile and skin that looked as if it would never tan.

"I've heard of you, Mrs. Maloney."

"Miss."

"Is that spelled *Ms?*"

"That stands for manuscript. Manuscripts are what Gregory Doyle deals in, among other things. I am here to ask about the investigation into the death of his wife."

"You're with Benjamin Rush, aren't you?"

"That's right."

"The fine hand of Sister Mary Teresa Dempsey. Do you expect to be defending Doyle?"

"Is he charged with something?"

"The prosecutor is mulling it over at this very moment."

"What prosecutor?"

"Julia Sirridge."

"Ouch."

"Amen. But then she may say ouch when she hears you are representing Doyle."

"What can you tell me?"

Irene took notes as he talked. He told it as he would have developed it for the prosecutor. A divorced man finally runs out of patience with a wife who has taken him for nearly everything he had. There had been talk of her marrying again and maybe that triggered it, but whatever, there was a good prima facie case against him and an arraignment looked sure.

"It's full of holes."

"So is Swiss cheese, but people buy it all the time."

DOYLE WAS A BIT of a surprise. He was busy when she entered his shop, and she had a chance to observe him for ten minutes before he was free. The answer he was giving his prospective customer, a man who kept his hat on as if to indicate he was just looking, suggested that Doyle had his didactic side. He knew a lot and he obviously liked to pass it along. What she did not notice was any sign that he was worried. Or any sign of grief, for that matter. What is the protocol on grieving for ex-spouses?

"May I help you?"

She put out her hand. "Irene Maloney. Mr. Benjamin Rush suggested that we talk."

He stepped back and surveyed her, registering a little surprise at her youth but not put off by it.

"I'm Bernadette Doyle's father."

"Of course! I never made the connection. How is she?" And then she stopped. "Good Lord, she discovered the body, didn't she?" Irene was not sure whether it was good or bad that she was acquainted with her client, if that was entirely accurate. She had seen Bernadette hardly at all since high school.

"Come in back. You heard the racket the door makes whenever anyone comes in." Irene had been more struck by the roaring vacuum a black woman was pushing around the shop.

"Back" was an office, beyond which she could see a workroom. The smell of pipe tobacco and leather permeated the room. When they were seated he picked up his pipe. "Do you mind?"

"It's your office."

There was enough lingering smoke to turn her into an addict, but she had quit during her second year of law school and convinced herself she didn't miss it a bit. If she took up smoking again she decided it would be a pipe.

"So," he said.

"I have read the papers, of course, and I have just come from the police. Why don't you tell me everything you know about your wife's death."

"You want to know if I killed her."

"Did you?"

"Would it matter? I mean, would you be my lawyer then?"

Irene felt a little frisson. She had never represented a confessed murderer. Was Gregory Doyle one? It was hard to get rid of the notion that those who kill are a race apart, somehow programmed to do things others would not do. She couldn't believe that. If killers are set off from the rest of the race, it is because they have actually done what others might well do if sufficiently provoked.

"Guilt or innocence is something decided by a trial."

"Will there be a trial?"

"I've talked to the police and they have made a presentation to the prosecutor. It is up to her."

"Her?"

"It's a changed world. Her name is Julia Sirridge and she makes Madame Defarge look like a guardian angel. If she goes for an indictment, it will be because she thinks she can win."

"What reason am I supposed to have for killing my wife?"

"That she's no longer your wife."

"We agreed to separate; we agreed to divorce; the settlement was mutually acceptable."

"And it didn't bother you that she intended to marry again?"

"She told me nothing about that."

"Did you talk regularly?"

"Yes."

"How often?"

"Once a week, often more."

"Really?"

"Irene, we were still pretty good friends."

"It was an inside job. Whoever killed your wife knew that house as well as his own."

"His?"

"The footprints the police were able to lift from the carpet, plus a pretty plain one in some spilled talcum powder, indicate a man. He was wearing some kind of rubber boot."

"Rubber boot?"

"Does that suggest someone to you?"

He shook his head, and for the first time she thought he was holding back.

"Sure?"

He nodded. Did he think it wasn't lying if he said nothing?

"Tell me about yourself."

He smiled. "There is very little to tell. Of late my life and my business have been pretty much the same thing. Fortunately, I like what I do."

"Books, isn't it?"

"Books. Finding them, selling them, restoring them, binding them. And reading them. It's a nice life."

He went on, and as she listened she was imagining him on the witness stand. Would a jury find him as plausible as she did, as Ben Rush had? Irene had no misgivings at all about defending him if it came to that—except for his odd reaction to the mention of boots.

TEN

A SURLY, INARTICULATE student was trying to explain to Geoffrey Stone why he should not have received a failing grade on his midterm exam.

"You failed to answer any question satisfactorily."

"Well, you know, just 'cause I don't agree with what you say, you know, don't mean I fail."

Stone sighed. "It's simply me against you, is that how you see it?"

Of course he did. He was a child of his age. Stone saw no reason to unload all his resentments on this poor kid. He told him to hang in there, he still had a chance to pull through. Of course he would give him a passing grade. No one failed anymore. It was as if the institution had accepted the relativism of the students. Worse, the notion that there are only opinions, no truths, that no opinion is better than another—such relativism had trickled into the streets from rarefied academic discussions that had been carried on at a time when there were still standards.

There were no standards anymore. Once a high school diploma certified to more knowledge than people receiving degrees today, even some advanced degrees, could be expected to have. Where would it all end? Practically speaking, a college education meant more than it ever had; but as far as content went, it was a joke.

No wonder Stone saw teaching only as providing the conditions for his private research, research that had nothing to do with the illiterate students he faced in the classroom. His visit to the house on Walton Street and his talk with Sister Mary Teresa Dempsey had galvanized him. Who would have thought that hidden away in that house and under that preposterous habit was a scholar diligently devoting herself day after day to the writing of her magnum opus? In the Dark Ages, monasteries had been bastions where some fragments of learning were retained. In the new Dark Ages, scholars were in diaspora, scattered. He saw the lecture series he had organized as a chance to make connections. And what a find was Sister Mary Teresa!

"Find?" said Allemagne of the Newberry. "My dear fellow, I put you on to her."

"And this continent was here before Columbus discovered it."

"Well, if discovery is going to mean only that something hitherto unknown to someone comes to be known by that someone, life becomes very exciting."

"She's agreed to go first. I think she will make the series. Her talk must be publicized widely. I want an enormous crowd."

"Spilling into the streets, scalping tickets for unheard-of amounts, a messy bit of trampling as they enter." Allemagne's view of the world was mordant and more dismal than Stone's.

And he stopped by the shop of Gregory Doyle, the book dealer the nun had mentioned, where a few odd volumes of Migne caught Stone's attention.

"Any authors you're particularly interested in?"

"Ramón Lull and Gersonides."

"The rector of the Sorbonne?"

"Not Gerson, Gersonides."

"Tell me about him."

How could he not like a man who listened with such obvious interest and curiosity? Doyle brought out some reference books and bibliographies, and soon he had a fix on Gersonides.

"Sister Mary Teresa Dempsey mentioned your place. I'm ashamed I didn't know of it."

"How do you know her?"

"I don't. I asked her to give a lecture in a series I'm organizing at the Newberry, and we got together to talk about that. I'd never known her before either."

Stone bought nothing on that visit. But he was given a tour of the place. Doyle showed him the leathers he had in stock. "For binding. I'm trying to get caught up."

That remark came back to Stone a few days later when he was leafing through the paper before going off to class and found himself looking into the smiling countenance of the book dealer. Gregory Doyle had been indicted for the murder of his former wife.

ELEVEN

MONSIGNOR HOOPER, pastor of St. Anne's, took charge of things, even going to the funeral home with Brian and Tom to make arrangements. Arrangements. Bernie begged off on that one. Ever since she had broken down while talking with Sister Kimberly, she no longer trusted her emotions. At any moment her protective external manner might desert her and she would be revealed for the bewildered little girl she felt herself to be. There was not the slightest reference by the pastor to the fact that her parents had divorced. Dad continued to be a conscientious Catholic, she knew that for a fact, and it drew attention to her own lost fervor. But she was a paragon of regularity compared to her mother.

"Of course I go to mass," she had replied indignantly when Bernie had once dared broach the subject. "I just don't do it by the numbers anymore."

"Just when you feel like it?"

"Are feelings such a poor guide?"

Her mother had stoppers like that, to which Bernie had no immediate answer. Besides, on this topic she had not been playing from strength, and she suspected her mother knew it.

"I gave you all good example when you were young. Just as you'll give good example when you start your family."

A little stiletto there; why weren't she and Augie producing babies? Her mother probably thought they had some surefire preventative, but the fact was they were anxious to have a child, were doing everything they knew how to have one. The suggestion that their marriage was just a liaison hurt. But then her mother meant to hurt her.

They had spent a lot of time hurting one another, and Bernie decided she liked Monsignor Hooper's blithe indifference to the way things stood between her mother and the Church. It was all between her and God now anyway, which had been her recent earthly claim as well.

"Priests are all well and good, and I can honestly say I never knew one I could not respect and admire. But they don't have much imagination, do they?"

If imagination was what made her mother leave her father, then divorce him, then reclaim the house that had been theirs, Bernie was ready to salute anyone who lacked it.

"WHY DID YOU ASK if I'd received a wedding invitation?" Brian inevitably asked.

The three of them, Brian, Tom and Bernie, were sitting in a bar on North Michigan. Music oozed from the pores of the place; a television mounted behind the bar shone through the gloom. It was good having a drink with her brothers.

Brian said, "Mom would have approved."

Tom said, "On the plane, I thought, I'll bet there are others on this flight making a sad trip. I suppose that's true of most flights."

"Most bars too, maybe."

Brian began to nod and then caught himself. "I'm serious. Look, we're practically orphans."

"How was Dad at the funeral parlor?"

"He left that to us."

"What was the deal about a wedding invitation?"

"The first story about what had happened mentioned that Mom was planning on marrying again."

"Come on."

"It's true."

"Who?"

"Does the name Philip Chesney Cord mean anything to you?"

They groaned in harmony as she pronounced the name with great precision. "Cecilia," Tom said, whistling as he did.

"Right."

Cecilia Cord had been—well, was—a friend of Bernie's. She had actually done her freshman year in Wisconsin and then transferred to Loyola, which had turned her down originally. Cece was small and round-eyed and very very cute. An only child, she'd made a pest of herself hanging around the Doyle household, marveling at such a big family, by which she meant the boys. Why is it that the attainable does not attract? Bernie was sure either of her brothers would have pursued Cecilia on a free-market basis, but to have her mooning about the house, obviously ready to be enthralled by either of them, granted her invisibility. Bernie tried to ease things along by having all four of them go out together, figuring maybe something might click, but it never had, and finally she realized she was glad. Imagine having Cecilia as a sister-in-law.

That newspaper story had brought back her mother's attitude to Cecilia. If Cece was enthralled by the Doyle household, Bernie's mom was gaga about the Cords. Their money went back several generations; they were prominent in Chicago society, members of several clubs besides the yacht club, with boxes at Soldier Field and Wrigley. The only reason Bernie had gotten to know her was because of a summer job at a tennis club the Cords belonged to. Cece must have noticed Brian or Tom come for her, and soon they were friends. Cecilia's father was tall, lean, bronzed with sun-bleached blond hair.

"A Greek god." Her mother sighed.

"Watch out then. We're reading the *Iliad* at school."

It was the first time Bernie had been embarrassed by her mother. A middle-aged woman mooning over someone else's father as if her own life weren't just about everything she could want. Even Lavinia seemed to notice it. Bernie felt she was revisiting a teenage version of herself, developing crushes now on this unknown boy, now on that. The feeling had little to do with its object; she didn't even know them, for crying out loud. It was a kind of private indulgence, daydreaming. A phase you went through, not a lifelong thing. Her mother had grown out of it—she must have; Bernie had never seen her act like this before—but now she was growing back into it. She began to ask Cece questions about her family, her mother, circling, circling, until she got to her father. What was he like? What does he do? How long has he been sailing? There was a time there when her mother nagged her father about buying a boat, but he knew enough to resist that one. "A hole in the water into which you shovel money," he said. "I am quoting."

"What are we saving for?"

"To put three kids through college."

That had been four or five years ago, more, and Bernie and Cece grew apart; she was now living in Denver with a husband Bernie had never even met, and if she visited her parents she didn't call. But it all seemed like yesterday when, still numb from the sight of the nude body of her mother with the great wound in her head, Kim told her of the newspaper account with its mention of the victim's planned marriage to Cece's father.

Her brothers knew nothing of their mother's girlish crush on Mr. Cord, and Tom wanted to know if he was the reason.

"For what?"

"For the separation and divorce."

Bernie shrugged. Maybe, but she doubted it. She could imagine her mother moving heaven and earth to come into the path of Philip Cord. "Oh, hi. Our daughters know one another. I'm Margaret Nelson. Margaret Nelson Doyle?"

She shivered in embarrassment at the image. But it was just as likely that her mother had never even met him and had told someone they were about to marry and that explained it. Only it didn't. "Sister Mary Teresa Dempsey received a printed invitation in the mail," Kim had said, and she had checked her mail and called the boys and nothing.

"Can we go to the house now?" Brian asked.

"You don't want to stay there, do you?"

"Why the hell not? Are we supposed to burn it down and salt the earth because of what happened?"

"We may have fun selling it."

"We?"

"Dad."

"Maybe he'll move back."

In the silence that followed, they might all have been thinking of the suspicion their father was under.

TWELVE

KATHERINE SENSKI suggested to Benjamin Rush that he invite her to lunch at his club, and he asked which one.

"Surprise me," she said coquettishly. "You choose."

He chose the Cliff Dwellers and waited until after their drinks came before looking questioningly at her.

"So what is this all about, Katherine?"

"Our mutual friend."

Benjamin Rush smiled at even so oblique a reference to Sister Mary Teresa. Well, the three of them were veterans of the effort to save the college and stop the frenzy with which a majority of the sisters were busily disposing of the order's property and distributing the proceeds to the poor. Since they had taken the vow of poverty, that included themselves as well. They set up in expensive North Shore apartments, they dressed indistinguishably from other well-to-do women, they signed statements and manifestos expressing solidarity with the poor and marginalized, and within a year and a half they had disappeared into the sea of the people. Thanks to

Benjamin Rush, the house on Walton Street had been saved—the fact that the donor, an alumna, had deeded it to Sister Mary Teresa provided the legal basis for that, even though Emtee Dempsey insisted she owned nothing; what was given to her was given to the Order of Martha and Mary.

"I'm just making sure the house stays in the possession of the order," Benjamin Rush had told her, and she figuratively looked the other way while he worked his legal magic. In the process, he had also rescued the property on the shore of Lake Michigan across the border in Indiana. They were victories that felt like defeats whenever the three of them pondered what had so recently been.

"What about our mutual friend?" Benjamin Rush said now, still smiling.

"It seems more and more certain that she alone received an invitation to the supposed impending marriage of Margaret Doyle and Philip Cord."

"What could she possibly have seen in him?" the lawyer asked. "He is a playboy, not in the usual sense but in the sense that he fritters away his life in recreation."

"He denies that any wedding was planned."

"I noticed that. I'm not surprised. Insisting on it seems ungallant, doesn't it?"

"He has an alibi."

The snow-white brows rose above the dark-rimmed glasses.

"He's in Paris for the French Open. Tennis."

"I can believe it. Wafting across the ocean to divert himself watching others play a silly game."

"All games are silly."

"Not golf."

Katherine tapped her glass with a nail, calling them to order. "We are getting off the subject."

"Which is?"

"Why should Sister and only Sister receive an invitation to an imaginary wedding?"

"You've been thinking of answers."

"I have been thinking that whoever singled her out could very well be the one who killed Margaret."

"And what is the significance of the invitation?"

"If I knew the answer to that, I wouldn't have let you talk me into having lunch with you."

Mainly what she wanted to do was to lodge in Benjamin Rush's mind what increasingly seemed to her a troubling fact. There was an invitation; she had seen it: twice. Sooner or later, it was bound to figure in any investigation of the murder. Katherine's paranoid fear was that the invitation was an effort to discredit Sister Mary Teresa Dempsey. She could not have told even Benjamin Rush of this, since that would make the murder of Margaret just an instrument for getting at Emtee Dempsey, and that did sound farfetched.

"I am going to the funeral," she said.

"You will take our mutual friend?"

"She refused. They have a car, she told me, and she has no wish to tie me down."

Rush closed his eyes at this reminder of the battered VW that was the sole vehicle owned by the Order of Martha and Mary. He had proposed buying them a more appropriate car but was firmly turned down.

"If the Order of Martha and Mary survives this near-fatal blow to its existence, it will be because the few of us left remain faithful to our vows. Poverty, chastity, and obedience."

"Whom do you obey?"

"The Blessed Abigail Keineswegs. By keeping the rule she wrote, I fulfill the third vow."

Katherine had witnessed this exchange and chided Emtee Dempsey for not permitting Benjamin Rush to perform an act of charity. The old nun ticked off half a dozen more worthy recipients of any generosity he wished to express.

"I will send my car around to take them."

"She will refuse."

"Not when I tell her that its funereal appearance makes it more appropriate to the occasion."

"What do you think of my worry about that invitation?"

"I share it. Have you spoken to the police?"

"They already know. Inspector Richard Moriarity has been told of the invitation."

"But did he consider the significance of its being the only one sent?"

"I shall speak to him," Katherine said resolutely.

"The police should have ways of finding out where it was printed."

THIRTEEN

WHEN SHE MAJORED in library science at the College of Martha and Mary, Shirley Loudon had an intimation that she was pointing herself in the direction of the single life, but then at the time she had seriously thought of entering the order. Thank God, she hadn't. Who then would have expected the chaotic events that followed on her graduation? Shirley had stayed right on campus, working in the college library, and always felt she had been an eyewitness to the end of the world, or at least what had been the world for many, herself included.

Margaret Nelson claimed not to be in the least surprised. "What's not getting married got to do with loving God?"

"What's marrying only one husband got to do with love?"

Margaret had wrinkled her nose. "You're imitating Emtee Dempsey. Only you don't make any sense."

But Shirley answered her own question with another. "What if you married and your husband had some awful accident and your future turned out to be only taking care of him?'' Such self-denial seemed the essence of true love.

"I'd put him in a home and go looking for another."

"Margaret!"

"Shirley, each of us has only one life to live, and I don't intend to waste mine."

"If I thought you were serious, I'd hate you."

Margaret threw her arms around her and laughed it all away, but even to say things like that revealed a disturbing side in her best friend. It mystified Shirley what Margaret Nelson saw in her. Margaret had a natural beauty that was breathtaking, but her manner was so easygoing that after a while you forgot how attractive she was.

"Why are we friends?" she asked Margaret once.

"What a question. Don't you like me?"

"Of course I like you."

"And I like you, and that's why we're friends. Besides, I like to shock you."

In those days, dances were arranged between the Catholic colleges in the Chicago area, and buses would take students from one to the other. This was particularly nice for a college like their own, a women's college, and acquaintances became friends and many later married. Shirley went to the dances when they were held at M&M, if only because Margaret teased her unmercifully until she did. That is how she met Gregory Doyle.

He looked about as uncomfortable as she felt, and it put her at ease trying to make him comfortable.

"I'm a lousy dancer."

"I'll be the judge of that." It was a line she might have borrowed from Margaret. She found herself adopting Margaret's persona with Greg, a fateful move.

But the night they met had been wonderful; she had never had such a good time with a man before. She didn't worry that he might at any moment start lunging at her, or doing things she wouldn't know how to handle. He was in every way a gentleman, yet he seemed genuinely attracted to her. They danced the few dances they danced together; they had a Coke and went for a walk on the campus.

"What's your library like?"

"Uneven. It's good in history."

That was Sister Mary Teresa's doing, of course. She was ruthless in her quest for acquisitions in her area and blamed the other professors for not paying more attention to the holdings in their own fields. Few students would read most of the books she had the library order. The joke was that there were more foreign language books in history than in foreign languages.

Greg told her he spent every moment he could in the used bookstores of Chicago and at estate sales, slowly building up a collection. "Not everyone knows the value of books. I sometimes worry about the morality of paying half a dollar for something I know is worth ten or fifteen or more."

He went to Goodwill and St. Vincent de Paul, both of which had huge book sections, something Shirley would never have guessed.

"And there are furniture stores."

"Furniture stores!"

He grinned. "It just struck me one day, the amount of books used as props in furniture stores. They want to make living room suites look homey, and how better than with a few books? The first store I really looked at I found a first edition of Jack London. Any relative?"

"My name's Loudon."

He cupped his ear and pretended not to hear. Shirley had never laughed so much at little things like that in her life.

"Who is he?" Margaret asked.

"Just someone I danced with."

"Is that why you dragged him off into the dark?"

"Margaret!"

But it was exciting to think of being held by Gregory Doyle, to imagine his lips on hers.

"You're blushing."

"For you, Margaret. You ought to be ashamed of yourself."

That night she lay in her dormitory bed and systematically reviewed in her mind every moment she had been with Gregory Doyle. If she had even thought of it then, the notion that she might become a nun would have seemed preposterous.

It was the only time she would have with Greg. She waited in the hope that he would call or write or something, but all she got was a message sent back through Margaret from another dance.

"Was he with someone?"

"I think he was looking for you."

So she got on the bus and went to the next dance and he wasn't there. She went to the next with the same results. The third dance she stayed home, and of course Margaret saw him.

"He's not much of a dancer."

"What did he have to say?"

"He didn't get a word in. My technique with boys is to dominate the conversation; that way they don't try anything unless I want them to."

Shirley was devastated at hearing such talk about such a man as Gregory Doyle. It hurt too to think of dazzling Margaret dominating him. She said nothing and it was a good thing because soon Margaret was getting calls from him, they were dating, and Shirley made a novena to St. Jude, patron of lost causes. Kneeling in chapel made her think again of a vocation. That was silly, of course, as if it were either Greg or God. She knew she had no claim on him. For heaven's sake, they had enjoyed a pleasant evening, had shared some interests, and that was that. Shirley told herself she was glad Margaret and Greg got along so well.

They made a handsome couple, and when she was in the bridal party Shirley wept with joy for the two of them and never had tears been so painful a pleasure. The college folded, Shirley joined the staff of the University of Chicago library, she and Margaret stayed in touch, but inevitably their different lives took them in different directions. Finally, it came down to carefully planned lunches downtown. Shirley always found an excuse not to accept invitations to Greg and Margaret's home.

Their friendship had been unexpectedly reactivated when Margaret called and invited Shirley to have dinner that very night with her at the Palmer House.

"My, my."

"I'm staying here."

"You are?"

"Come and I'll tell you all about it."

She could hardly fail to accept so enigmatic an invitation. If Margaret had sounded a little tense on the phone, she was a vision when she emerged from the elevator, her dress swirling about her as if she were Venus rising from the sea.

"Shirl!" she cried and they embraced with a fervor that added to the mystery.

They had drinks in the lobby first, to people-watch and, as Shirley later saw, to ease into the big revelation. It came as soon as they had ordered and the waiter had taken away their menus.

"Greg and I are separating."

Shirley just looked at her. Since it couldn't be a serious remark, she sat there waiting for Margaret to say more. As a joke, it lacked everything, but it had to be a joke.

"Well, say something for heaven's sake."

"I don't believe it."

"And I don't blame you. Who would have thought I'd have the nerve after all those years in the same rut?"

"That isn't what I mean."

It didn't matter what she had meant. Margaret was in full flow now, describing the thwarting years during which she had devoted herself entirely to Greg and the kids, leaving nothing for herself.

"What about me? That's what I asked myself, and there wasn't any answer I liked. Shirl, I have to act now or it will be too late."

"Too late for what?"

"To be *me*. You ought to understand that. You've been a model to me, Shirley, a woman who set her own course and has done what she decided to do."

Shirley was appalled at this selfish interpretation of how she lived. She might have told Margaret that she in turn was her model for what a fulfilled life would be like. To be successful, as she was, was nice, but it wasn't everything. It was, finally, very very lonely. She had grown used to that, but she would have preferred not to have needed to. If Margaret was the woman she would have preferred to be, it was largely because of Greg.

"What does Greg say to all this?"

"You know Greg."

"I *knew* Greg. Years ago."

"Basically, he agrees with me."

"He feels stunted too?"

"It's different with men. His only concern was who would clean up after him. So we agreed to share Lavinia."

"What exactly do you want to do?"

Margaret sat forward, eyes sparkling. Her beauty had kept pace with her age; she was if anything more attractive now. Shirley wondered if that is what Margaret wanted, to attract men.

"That's the point of it. I don't have to live according to some predictable schedule. I want to be free of that. I want to explore."

Shirley had the feeling she was listening to clichés, though she had never been involved as confidante in anything resembling this. Margaret must be going through a phase. It happened at their age. Maybe a few days in a hotel room would be cure enough.

"Have you talked with Sister Mary Teresa?"

"Yes!"

"And?"

"Well, you know what she'd say, what she'd have to say."

"So you came to me?"

"Yes." The hand she put on Shirley's was her left. Her engagement and wedding rings sparkled in the restaurant lights.

Shirley listened. That, in the circumstances, seemed the thing to do. Just listen. Margaret would have heard home truths about what she was doing from Sister Mary Teresa, and the nun could speak them with authority. With Shirley, Margaret wanted an opportunity for an uncriticized outpouring of her feelings.

Driving home it occurred to Shirley that if Margaret left Greg then Greg would be free. She called him the following day.

"Greg? Shirley Loudon. I had the most incredible conversation with Margaret last night."

"What do you think?"

"I think she's out of her mind."

"That's the result of all these years of marriage."

"You're taking it calmly enough."

"It takes two to tango, Shirley."

Tell me, she thought. She wasn't the wimp she'd been when Margaret waltzed off with Gregory, the guy Shirley had found. "I thought if we talked we could figure out the approach I should take. Last night, I lent an ear and that was about it."

"Come to the store."

Had she been unaware all these years how Greg supported his family? The store came as a surprise, even if it was a kind of busman's holiday for her, ohing and ahing over his books, but then he showed her his workshop, and it was clear that he had devised a career that was a combination of profitable enterprise and what he would do for nothing if it came to that. Was Margaret jealous of Greg's justifiable content with what he had accomplished?

They stayed there in the store, and in some ways their conversation was like the first one they'd had all those years ago. Once more Shirley felt an affinity with him that put her at ease in a way she seldom was with people. But haunting the scene was Margaret. And inescapable was Greg's love for his wife. She was not simply a beautiful woman, the woman to whom he had pledged his life, she was the mother of their children, the other half of his soul. Any predatory thoughts Shirley had had in seeking him out dissipated as they talked. She was used to sacrificing her own feelings. She resolved to do everything she could to bring Margaret and Greg back together again.

But nothing she did helped at all. Margaret continued to think of her as somehow her co-conspirator in all this.

"Margaret, he loves you."

"Of course he does. And I love him. That isn't in question."

"But you're putting it in question. You're saying you want to live apart from him, not with him. Is that love?"

"You don't understand."

What Shirley was taken not to understand was that to have a husband and three wonderful children, to have started a prospering travel agency, to have a freedom she had never had before—none of that meant anything when put beside Margaret's amorphous desire for something more. It was difficult remaining patient with her when she could not say what that something was.

"Do you want other men, is that it?"

"Would that be so awful?"

"Margaret!"

"No, I mean it. Sister Mary Teresa gave me the vale-of-tears stuff. But that's my point. Life is so short and I have seen so very little of it. What's the point of being alive if you're only allowed a sliver of life?''

It was far worse than Shirley had imagined. She went to see Sister Mary Teresa. Whatever Margaret said, it was obvious that what the old nun thought about what she was doing mattered a lot to her. And on Walton Street she had received absolutely no sympathy.

''Emotionally, she's what she was in college,'' Sister Mary Teresa said. ''Do you know Kierkegaard's *Either/Or?* No? You should read it. In volume one there is a section called Diapsalmata, effusions of emotion on the part of a young man: high, low, joy, despair, completely out of rational control. It's a phase many go through, but Margaret seems never to have gotten through it. How could she have been a good wife all these years?''

''And she was. I talked with Greg.''

''I have waited for him to bring it up.''

''You know him?''

''He sells books.''

''Of course.''

''What we are doing for her is praying.''

Shirley was reminded of the novena she had made in the college chapel. All prayers are answered, but sometimes the answer is no.

''Something has to jolt her out of it.''

But nothing did. It got worse. Separation was only make-believe, she wasn't really on her own. Anytime she wanted to go home, she could; that was the agreement with Greg, but that made a joke of her independence. She filed for divorce.

"Margaret, you're a Catholic."

"Right. So we know a divorce doesn't undo a marriage, it's just a legal thing."

Shirley became annoyed at Greg's acquiescence in the divorce.

"It's not like an annulment."

"I don't think you really care what she does."

"Love has to be freely given, Shirley. That's what makes marriage such a risk. Two people have to go on freely loving one another."

She could have cried. She could have screamed at him. My God, he had his rights as a husband! He should go and just grab her.... Here her imagination deserted her, but her breath caught at the image of being swept up in his arms and mastered by him.

Wasn't it predictable that when the divorce went through it would affect Margaret's notion of where she stood vis-à-vis Greg? When they lunched, Shirley became aware of how much on display Margaret was, though her eyes never wandered. She seemed to be presenting herself to whom it might concern. The next step in her romantic adventure was inevitable.

"He sails, he's always in the paper. You must have heard of him."

"Philip Cord?"

"Of course you have."

"Are you seeing him?"

"Shirley, he doesn't know I exist. Yet." And she picked up her glass of chablis and sipped it, a significant look in her eye.

Another man would mean the definitive death of Margaret's marriage to Greg, Shirley was convinced of this. Something had to be done. Something dramatic. Something that would bring Sister Mary Teresa onto center stage. If anyone could put a stop to Margaret's reckless romanticism it was Sister Mary Teresa Dempsey.

After hours, on the computer at the library, using a desktop publishing program, she devised an invitation to the wedding of Margaret Nelson Doyle and Philip Chesney Cord. The Methodist church was an inspiration. She ran the text off on the laser printer and took the camera-ready copy to an instant printer who specialized in invitations.

"As a proof?" the ponytailed boy behind the counter said, looking past her.

"But make it exactly the way the finished product will look.

He did, and she mailed it off to Sister Mary Teresa and waited for the fireworks to begin. Margaret

would be summoned to Walton Street and given the
lecture of her life. She would deny any intention to
marry, she would no doubt guess who had devised
the invitation, but, Shirley decided, at bottom this
was an essentially friendly act. She wanted to prevent Margaret from doing something irreparable.

FOURTEEN

SISTER MARY TERESA in her flamboyant habit suggestive of an earlier day caused a sensation as she came down the main aisle of St. Anne's Church, making audible use of her cane. Kim followed a pace behind. Any effort to help Emtee Dempsey would have been rebuffed. She refused to be treated like a child or, rather, like the old woman she was. The day before, Kim had taken her to the funeral home before the official wake began, and the old nun had stood beside the casket looking down at her former student and tears stood in her eyes.

"All she wanted was God. He is all anyone wants, no matter the odd places we seek him. Now she has found him."

Emtee Dempsey did not attribute the oddities of Margaret's later life to any deadly moral flaw; it was only weakness.

"That's what the moral life is, Sisters," she had said to Kim and Joyce. "Adjusting to our weaknesses."

Her spiritual conferences, one of her tasks as their superior, came at odd moments and seemed informal, but what she said stayed in the mind. Kim could see that the old nun hoped against hope that she and Joyce were the seeds of rebirth of the order rather than its last members.

The usher had taken them to the second pew from the front, just behind that reserved for the family. There was a black woman already in the pew, and she looked with alarm at Sister Mary Teresa. The old nun introduced herself in an audible whisper. The black woman identified herself as Lavinia, who had been the Doyles' cleaning lady for years. In a few minutes, they stood while in the back of the church Monsignor Hooper began the rite. Then the pallbearers wheeled the casket to the front of the church, the family following. As he entered the pew in front of them, following his sons and daughters, Gregory Doyle nodded to Sister Mary Teresa. Bernadette had put her hand on Kim's as she went by.

Monsignor Hooper performed his tasks with a fixed smile and, at every point in the liturgy when it was possible, referred with great unction to the deceased and to those she had left behind. Eulogies had once been out of place at Catholic funerals, and Emtee Dempsey began to stir at this personalizing of the liturgy. On the drive over in Benjamin Rush's car she had gone on about what a great mistake dropping the requiem mass had been.

"If it is permitted, that is what I shall want. Above all, the Dies Irae, sung by a melancholy baritone.

The Christian trust in the Resurrection is not meant to negate the dread reality of death. Without it, there is no contrast.''

Katherine Senski had shaken off the suggestion that she join them in the pew behind the family.

"I'll sit with Shirley Loudon," she said, looking around and picking the first person she recognized.

"Have her come too."

But Katherine had swept off, and they went up the aisle without her. Their usual worship was private and intense: on Walton Street, when they had a priest to say mass in their chapel; even at the cathedral in the early morning, when Father McHugh, an old priest who worked in the chancery, said a seven o'clock mass. It was Emtee Dempsey's project to secure him as their chaplain when he retired. Father McHugh was willing but the cardinal had expressed some vague thoughts about the continuing of an order with only three members, so it would have to be handled delicately. Kim found the funeral mass in this huge and ornate parish church a constant barrage of distractions.

Gregory Doyle knelt erectly, sat straight-backed, or stood almost at attention as the liturgy required, and Kim had the sense that he was making a heroic effort to restrain his emotions. Next to him, Bernadette was weeping silently and her two brothers seemed bewildered by what had happened. Mean-

while, Monsignor Hooper went on as if they had all
been living under the same roof until the other
morning, when tragedy struck the Doyle household.

Outside the church, Emtee Dempsey fell into conversation with Lavinia, the black cleaning lady. Since
Benjamin Rush's car was at their disposal still, the
sisters went to the cemetery taking Katherine and
Shirley Loudon with them, two and two on facing
seats in the extended car. Lavinia, wide-eyed, had
refused to join them.

"Did the pastor know the family?" Katherine
asked, her brows lifted. "Did he know what Margaret had been up to?"

"De mortuis nil nisi bonum."

"What's it mean?"

"Et tu, Katherine? Translate for her, Shirley."

And Shirley did, reduced by the tone of Emtee
Dempsey's voice to the status of student.

"I was talking about the priest, not Margaret
Doyle." Katherine sniffed and looked out the window.

Kim noticed that Shirley Loudon was taking short
breaths, and suddenly she was crying. A great sob
escaped her and then she buried her face in her
handkerchief, shaking her head violently, as if apol-
ogizing for this display. Emtee Dempsey reached
across and patted Shirley's knee. The librarian put
her hand over the old nun's and tried to stop the flow

of tears. She looked as bewildered as Margaret's sons at what had happened to her old schoolmate.

Shirley Loudon was not someone Kim knew well. In the past year or so she had stopped by to talk to Sister Mary Teresa, but Kim had the impression that the librarian was not as close or devoted to Emtee Dempsey as were other former students, even Margaret Doyle. And this was odd, since her profession was one that should have provided a closer bond between them. Shirley had never married and that might have been it. Like most religious, Emtee Dempsey had to feel part of a family, somehow connected with the continuation of the race. For Kim it was Richard's family. But Shirley was as cut off from all that as they were. Her grief now suggested that it had been the Doyle family to which she had attached herself.

"Shirley," Emtee Dempsey said in a firm voice, clearly meant to shake the librarian out of the doldrums. "Had Margaret spoken to you of intending to marry again?"

"You received an invitation."

"Did you?"

"No. No one else did. There was only the one. I sent it."

Benjamin Rush's car was soundproof, but even so a silence fell after what Shirley had said.

"You sent it?"

"Yes."

"Did Margaret ask you to?"

A shake of the head that caused her pageboy to swirl and then return impeccably in place. "It was my idea."

"But why? She had no intention of marrying that man, did she?"

Katherine's mouth was turned down and her brows raised.

"No. But she was trying to get to know him, to make something happen. I wanted you to stop her, and the invitation was meant to stir you up."

Emtee Dempsey's hands were now atop the handle of her cane. She said nothing as she considered what Shirley had told her.

"You didn't tell Margaret you were going to do this?"

"No, Sister, but I urged her to come see you. She'd told me the divorce was just a legal matter, that her marriage to Greg could not be dissolved, but then she began to talk about other men, especially Philip Cord. She was infatuated with him."

Emtee Dempsey sighed. "Well, thank God you've cleared that up."

"In the end it wasn't even necessary."

"Did Gregory Doyle know about her feelings for this man?"

Again a silence. "I don't know."

"Then you didn't mention it to him?"

"Oh, I could never have done that."

"It will make a good deal of difference to the police whether or not he knew."

"Oh, they can't imagine he would have done such a thing."

Katherine caught Kim's gaze. Her eyes rolled upward. Poor Katherine, she and her junior colleague Laura Cousins were out on a limb. Shirley could tell Richard what she had done, but he would see it as merely diversionary. The question would not be whether or not Gregory Doyle knew about a counterfeit invitation but whether he thought that what the invitation announced was true.

Emtee Dempsey invited Katherine and Shirley back to Walton Street for luncheon.

"Sister Joyce will be expecting you," she said, dismissing their demurs, and in a sense she was right. Joyce always expected the unexpected when Emtee Dempsey was out on an excursion.

"Richard called," she said to Kim.

"Did he leave a message?"

"A number."

It was neither his home number nor his office number, but it seemed somehow familiar. She dialed it.

"Doyle's."

"Mr. Doyle?" Kim was surprised. She would have imagined he would have spent time with his children after the funeral. "This is Sister Kimberly. I received a call from my brother and he left this number."

"I'll put him on."

Joyce moved around the kitchen, putting the final touches to the lunch she had indeed readied, but Kim knew her ears were sensitive antennae. No need to tell her whom she had reached.

"Kim?"

"Yes."

"Is she there?"

There was no mistaking the object of the question. "We have guests."

"I am calling her as a favor to Doyle. I'll give you the message. Gregory Doyle has confessed to the murder of his divorced wife, Margaret."

FIFTEEN

IRENE MALONEY WAITED in the counselor's visiting room, her long-fingered hands splayed on the top of her briefcase as if she were about to play a dirge. One of the worst things that can happen to an attorney had happened to her, and she was waiting to talk with the client who had done it. When Gregory Doyle appeared in the doorway, he looked at her with the same affability with which he greeted customers in his store.

"You've heard." He sat down across from her.

"Yes. I would have preferred to hear it from you."

"I want to plead guilty."

"You can't. On a charge this serious, it's all but impossible to escape a jury trial."

"What's there to try? I've admitted I did it."

"Why?"

The corners of his mouth dimpled slightly. "To get it over with, I guess. Why put so many people to so much trouble proving it when I could put an end to that?"

"You told them you killed your wife?"

He nodded.

"You picked up a marble statuette and hit her on the back of the head as she came naked from the bathroom?"

"Yes."

She didn't believe him. Before, when he asked if she would defend him if she knew he was guilty, she had felt a little shiver, but that was a response to an abstract possibility. She had never thought he had killed his wife, nor did she think the police thought so. They were anxious as always to get a case off their books and into the courts, emptying the ocean with a spoon: The tide of crime came inexorably in. She saw her role as ensuring that this understandable zeal did not infringe on her client's rights.

"Why did you kill her?"

"She had left me."

"I thought you agreed to that."

"I did. I thought that after some time by her-self..."

"She would return to you?"

"I was wrong. She then filed for a divorce."

"Uncontested. The settlement was generous to a fault. One might think you were anxious to get rid of her."

"No."

"You loved her?"

He sat back, closed his eyes for a moment, then sat forward. "Yes, of course I did. She was my wife."

"You killed her because you loved her?"

"'Each man kills the things he loves; the coward does it with a kiss, the brave man with a sword.'"

"Or with a marble statuette."

"Miss Maloney, I know this puts you in a spot but, forgive me, that was not the important thing. I don't want you to represent me anymore. I won't need a lawyer now."

"You'll need one more than ever. I am serious that Judge Droit won't let you plead guilty to murder. I'm going to plead you innocent."

"But I've already confessed to the police."

"Innocent by reason of insanity."

He reacted as if she had struck him. He had told the police he was guilty of murdering his wife, but the thought that he would sit in court as a mental incompetent shook him.

"I am not insane."

"That is what the prosecutor will try to prove."

"He'll have no problem."

"She."

"That's right. You told me."

When she left him, he had not repeated his statement that he did not want her to be his lawyer. If she would plead him as insane, she would need the agreement of the next of kin that she should represent him. That meant talking to the children. To Bernadette.

Bernadette did not know she was a lawyer, but then Irene did not know her old friend was a golf pro.

"Wasn't tennis your game?"

"I married the golf coach."

Irene widened her eyes and smiled. She wasn't jealous, she had made a decision: marriage either later or not at all. She was a career woman. And she had come here to talk to Bernadette about her father.

"I thought Badin was his lawyer."

"Benjamin Rush, the founder of the firm for which I work, asked me to talk to your father. I did. Along with Mr. Badin, who told your father that his law practice did not make him the obvious choice for what might happen if the prosecutor sought an indictment against him."

"Have you talked with him today?"

"I just left him."

"How did they get him to say such a thing?"

"I'm afraid he did it on his own."

"Can I see him?"

"I was about to suggest that you accompany me downtown now."

They sat on metal chairs at a metal table shaded by a festive green umbrella with white fringe. Birds swooping by, a light steady breeze, the smells of summer, the whirr of a hedge trimmer as a sullen

man trimmed the border of the practice green—
Irene felt she was taking Bernadette away from Eden
into the sinful city. Her smooth skin was weathered
and there was a perpetual squint in her eyes, as if she
were watching a drive.

"Why did he do it, Irene?"

"Kill your mother?" Irene's heart sank as she
asked it.

"No!" The slate-blue eyes turned full upon her.
"He didn't do that. He couldn't have. *I* could have
killed her, maybe, but he never could have."

"Why do you say that?"

"That I could have killed her?"

"Okay."

"Because of the way she treated my father. He is
one of the gentlest, most loving men I know, yet she
convinced herself that being married to him had
thwarted her life. At her age she decided to make up
for it. And he humored her. He let her leave home
and live on her own; he even went along with the divorce. Why did he think she wanted a divorce, for
God's sake?"

"Why did she?"

"Because she wanted adventure, sexual adventure, men. She was like a goddamn kid." Tears
sparkled in her angry eyes. "Boris," she snapped,
turning toward the man who had been moving closer

and closer as he trimmed the hedge. "Could you please not do that now?"

The man did not reply. He turned off the machine and began to gather up its electric cord in great looping coils, then shuffled resentfully away.

"Who is he?" Irene asked.

"Our Polish joke."

"I told your father that his actions suggest he wanted to get rid of her, that her desire to leave was convenient for him."

"What did he say?"

"He was sure she would come back."

"I think he was. Meanwhile, look at the way he lived. He always worked too hard; now he does nothing else. And where he lives? It's awful, and there she was all by herself in that great big house. Can you imagine what all her antics *cost* him? I mean the money. They were well off once."

"Didn't your mother have a business?"

"The travel agency? That was a device to get discounts for her own travel. She helped a few friends. The place was open only a few days a week, half days. It wasn't serious."

"What about your mother and Philip Cord?"

"She made it up."

"Did your father know about that?"

"I hope not." Her now dry eyes came back to Irene. "And not because I think he would have harmed her. It would have hurt him so much. God, how she hurt him!''

''Why do you think he'd say he did such a thing if he didn't?''

''Why *do* people confess to things they haven't done?''

''Many reasons.''

''Crazy as it seems, I think he may have blamed himself for my mother's actions, as if he had somehow let her down. Maybe it's some kind of reparation.''

But of course the reason people confess to crimes they haven't committed, when this isn't due to mental imbalance, is usually because they are trying to protect someone else they think did it.

''Tell me again what you found that morning at your mother's house. And try to think of anything that would show your father's story is false.''

There was a rehearsed tone to Bernadette's account, but of course she had told it now so many times she would be remembering what she had said as much as what she had seen. The bedroom when she entered it was so torn up that she noticed the open drawers, the things thrown onto the floor, the emptied closets, before she saw the body of her mother. On her way up the stairs she hadn't noticed signs of anyone's passage, the damp marks of the boots, nor had she noticed the boot print in the spilled talcum.

"By then I was screaming. Terrified. And I got out of there because for all I knew whoever had done that to her was still in the house."

"But there was no car in the drive?"

"No."

"How would someone get to the house otherwise?"

The back lawn abutted on a thirty-yard-deep strip of wilderness that ran between the residential lots and the tennis club beyond, a buffer of sorts, a kind of nature refuge.

"When we were kids we used to scare one another with stories of creepy monsters coming out of those woods."

What creepy monster had come out of the woods the morning Margaret Nelson Doyle had been so cruelly killed as she came from her bath?

SIXTEEN

KATHERINE SENSKI called from the house on Walton Street and asked Laura Cousins if she'd heard the news about Gregory Doyle.

"What news?"

"Then you haven't. No one else should have this yet either. He has confessed to the murder of his wife."

"Wow."

"This will make up for the supposed wedding."

"Supposed."

"I have the explanation of that. It will take us off the hook, but not enough. This scoop should restore you in Wilson's sights."

At least she had said "us." Laura checked this out before writing the story, feeling bad about that; Katherine Senski was everything Laura hoped to be as a reporter. She discovered a not insignificant detail. Gregory Doyle had been arrested before he confessed to murdering his wife.

"What made him do it?"

Inspector Richard Moriarity was always especially helpful because he hoped to enlist her in some kind of campaign against Sister Mary Teresa and the nuns on Walton Street.

"You know Katherine Senski?" he'd asked a few weeks ago.

"Of course."

"You're her protégée."

She felt like St. Peter, denying it, but she didn't like the suggestion that she was not her own woman. His wish to neutralize Katherine and her old friend was expressed in the most complicated of circumlocutions. She gathered that, if she kept him current on what Katherine was doing, he would cooperate with her in a way that would be very helpful to her career. It was duplicitous to let him believe that they were allies of a sort.

"I don't like the way she's always getting my sister, my real sister, Kimberly, mixed up in things that are none of their business."

The general grip took on specificity with the death of Margaret Nelson Doyle.

"You see?" he said. "They'll do it to you too. Feeding you that phony invitation." He made a noise by fluttering his lips. "Those two old dolls are trouble, take my word for it."

Now, when she asked what had prompted Doyle to confess, he smiled. "We have some noncircumstantial evidence."

"What is it?"

He settled back. "What did we have up until now? Someone who had easy access to the house, most likely someone with a key. Gregory Doyle had a key. Someone who knew exactly where he was going once he got into the house. Gregory Doyle. Someone with a motive. The slain woman had been giving Gregory Doyle a bad time for years, and her conduct could be construed as humiliating him, with talk of remarriage the final straw. They're both Catholic. Not much, you'd say, and you'd be right. What we know is consistent with Doyle's doing it, but it really doesn't prove anything."

"And now you have something that does?"

"Right. There was a boot print in some spilled talcum powder. We've got the boots. They were in Doyle's workroom behind his shop, stuffed in the back of a closet."

"Wow."

"That wasn't exactly his reaction. He sat right where you're sitting, just thinking, and then he said, 'I want to confess. I killed my wife.'"

"Exact words?"

"Verbatim."

"Was there blood or anything like that on the boots?"

He nodded in approval of the question. "We're going over them now. It would help but it isn't necessary. We've found a similar print in the woods behind the house, so he must have come in that way.''

"What kind of boots are they exactly?''

"Rubber pullover boots, the kind farmers and laborers wear in mucky weather.''

"Black, white, what?''

"Yellow. Red soles.''

She got it down, she thanked him, they were just old pals. In her car, stalled in traffic, she asked herself if a man who returns from killing his wife would stash those boots where anyone could find them. Why not? Why would he think they would incriminate him?

The point that stuck in her mind was that the killer had come to the house through the woods in back. Doyle might have done that to avoid being seen by the neighbors, he might have done that if he was trying to create a track for a supposed intruder. But then he would have thought of the boots.

Where do you buy boots like that?

SEVENTEEN

KOTARSKI SEEMED to have more joints than other people. When he sat it was like watching a camel kneel. Limbs bent in odd ways; he seemed to be placing himself in the chair. The chair was in the modest living room of the modest apartment in which the eminent scholar lived. He had agreed on the phone to take part in Geoffrey Stone's lecture series; he had, he permitted himself to say, a rather extraordinary announcement to make. Stone had come by El and taxi to find out what Kotarski meant.

Two days had intervened since the phone call, and Stone had been trying unsuccessfully to put the reedy, excited voice out of his mind. What if it was some lost fragment of a work, some hitherto unknown text in Greek philosophy? Kotarski had made his name as a scholar by adding six certain and three contested passages to the Aristotelian dialogue Gryllus, the fruit of a systematic thirty-year poring over the Greek fathers and the manuscripts on which the printed editions of them were based. None of this would make a headline in the *Chicago Tribune*, but something like that would be dynamite as a lecture. Stone could imagine future scholars referring to Kotarski's lecture in the Stone series at the Newberry Library. His chest constricted with excitement. That would be immortality indeed.

"A whishkey?"

"It's early."

"Or late." Kotarski showed teeth yellowed by decades of cigarette smoke. Outside of libraries, he was never without his cigarette holder, which he used so that he could smoke one hundred percent of a cigarette. When he was finished he shook a little ash from the holder as one might empty a pipe. Stone wondered if Kotarski had already had a "whishkey." "We must drink to my great discovery."

Stone disliked whiskey even at more appropriate hours of the day, but he did not want to offend his grinning host by suggesting an alternative libation. Kotarski chuckled as he poured bourbon into two cloudy glasses. They might have been kids behind the barn, doing something naughty out of sight of the adults.

"Prosit," Kotarski said, and tossed off an ounce and a half of bourbon as if it were water. Stone sipped his tentatively and put it on the table. A mistake. Kotarski topped off his guest's glass and refilled his own.

"Cheers," said Stone gloomily. He held his glass in his hands after another sip. He could feel it run

down his gullet; it might have been a dye given prior
to x-ray.

"A lifetime of work has come to a happy conclu-
sion."

"I am dying to hear what you have discovered."

"You know the Ambrosiana in Milan, of course."

"Of course."

"And Gabriel's catalog of the scientific manuscripts?"

"I have heard of it."

"It is rare. I own it." He put out a long arm that
plucked a book from the shelf as claws pick up
gumballs in a machine. Kotarski drained his glass,
put it on the table, and opened the book.

Kotarski's nicotine-stained finger pointed to entry 524, with the shelf mark E 151 Sup. A Latin
manuscript of the twelfth century that contained a
defective version of Rutilius Taurus Palladius' *De
agricultura.* Kotarski had a similar manuscript but
one which had what the Ambrosiana was missing.

"I have compared my manuscript with a microfilm of the Ambrosiana text, supplied by Dr. Louis
Jordan of Notre Dame. There are variations I have
mentioned; the one is not a copy of the other; if the
one is authentic so is the other."

"And where is the manuscript?"

Kotarski, eyes sparkling over his yellow smile, screwed a cigarette into his nicotine-stained holder, put it between his teeth, still smiling, and lit up.

"I own it."

"Own it? But how is that possible?"

In Stone's experience, manuscripts were owned by libraries, by institutions, by universities and religious orders, by museums, not by individuals, not by someone of limited means like Kotarski, who had bisected his mouth with a long yellowish finger.

"Was it stolen?"

"Works of art have been the object of plunder, theft, transportation, confiscation by a colonial power." Kotarski warmed to his subject. "The Ambrosiana itself had its origins in some items of rather dubious provenance. You will have read Angelo Paredi's memoir."

Was Kotarski saying he had purchased the manuscript from someone whose ownership of it was questionable? Stone began to wonder what kind of immortality a connection with Kotarski's discovery would give him.

"I see you are worried, my friend. Fear not. I am the rightful possessor of the manuscript, and I acquired it in a perfectly legal way from one who owned it."

"Is it here?" Stone spoke in hushed tones. Kotarski's messy apartment would be made almost holy by the presence in it of so rare and priceless a treasure.

"It is not here." His arm went out for the bottle, and he splashed another dollop in each of their glasses. This was clearly one of those moments when friends don't let friends drive, but then Kotarski had no car and they were friends only in the loosest sense. "I have had a microfilm made, and now some restoration work on the manuscript itself is in process."

Kotarski unfolded himself, stood, gained control of the floor, and shuffled out of the room telling Stone to follow. In another cluttered room stood a microfilm reader of the first generation, a huge upturned funnel of a machine, under which the head of the scholar went like a candle about to be snuffed. Kotarski flipped the switch, and a scratched screen was illuminated. The film was already on spools and threaded through the machine. Kotarski made some adjustments.

"Sit down, my friend. Look. This is an historic moment."

And so it was. Forget the drunken dramatics of Kotarski, Stone was looking at a genuine find.

"Congratulations, Professor."

"Thank you, Professor."

They actually shook hands. Kotarski turned off the machine, removed the microfilm, and put it in a box bearing the label of a Chicago firm.

"When can I see the original?"

"My plan is to show it at the time of my lecture. Security at the Newberry is sufficient, is it not?"

"You need have no fear. Once it is there."

Kotarski was busy with another cigarette.

"I suppose you sent it away for the restoration work."

"No. My dear Stone, there is a local man who is better than most so-called restoration experts with whom I have dealt. I had no hesitation in the world to put my manuscript into his hands."

They had returned to the living room. Stone picked up his glass and emptied it. What the hell, he wasn't driving either. His original elation at Kotarski's discovery had given way to a sullen envy. Why this chain-smoking pack rat of a man rather than himself? Imagine having such a treasure, to find it, to be able to buy it, to own it! The most Kotarski would say is that a Franciscan from Poland had approached him with the manuscript, his being the only name in Chicago his Franciscan community knew, owing to the fact that a second cousin of Kotarski was a member of that community. Let him gloat, Stone told himself, not bothering to wave off the bottle when Kotarski poured out another. The thought came to him with an almost audible popping.

"You said a local restorer?"

A grinning nod.

"Gregory Doyle?"

Kotarski laughed with delight. "Of course you would know him."

Stone looked around. There were no newspapers, no television, no radio. The cluttered room in which Kotarski worked had been equally devoid of indications of what century it was. Stone tried not to take pleasure in what he felt he must tell Kotarski.

"Doyle has been arrested, Professor Kotarski. He has confessed to the murder of his wife. He is in jail."

Kotarski's smile went like a snowflake hitting warm ground. He rose from his chair, a section at a time, seeming to inflate as he did. His eyes burned with some passion Stone could not identify.

"No!" roared Kotarski. "It cannot be!"

EIGHTEEN

SISTER MARY TERESA WAS in a foul mood. The terrible death of her former student was a tragedy, and difficult as tragedy is, it can be borne. The wedding invitation she had received and which had formed the basis of the story about the slaying had been explained. Shirley Loudon had acted foolishly, but there are worse things than folly. The police had proceeded as if the murderer were Gregory Doyle, which was stupid, but stupidity is an integral component of the human scene. Now Gregory Doyle had confessed to the murder, and this was a mystery. Outside of her religion, Emtee Dempsey had a low tolerance of mystery.

"Why?" the old nun asked.

"Jealousy? Because his love for her was despised?"

The headdress tipped and a cold blue eye fixed on Kim. "Why did he confess to a crime he did not of course commit?"

"Why of course?"

"There is one piece of evidence that connects Mr. Doyle to these dreadful events, a pair of boots. These boots were easily found when the man's workshop was searched. To say they were hidden because they were in a closet is nonsense. If he were hiding them because he thought they were incriminating he would not have put them there. He would have gotten rid of them. The boots were put there in the expectation that they would be found."

She picked up her fountain pen and moved it several inches to the left on her desk blotter.

"Of two things, one. Either someone put them there so the police would find them or *he* put them there with the same intention."

"That they be found."

"Yes. So either he is being framed or his confession is a redundancy. Putting the boots in the closet, if he did it, was meant to bring about his accusation for murder."

"There is another possibility. Someone else put the boots in the closet *and* he confessed to the murder."

Emtee Dempsey smiled for the first time that day, a radiant, eye-twinkling smile that seemed to light up the room. She brought her pudgy hands together in a soft slap.

"Exactly! And why would he do that?"

She seemed to be waiting for Kim to answer, but the part of prudence was to remain silent after one had said something that pleased the old nun.

"To pro-tect some-one." And she brought her hands together again.

If Bernadette O'Brien had called at that precise moment and asked to see Sister Mary Teresa, Kim would not have been surprised. As it was, an hour or two passed before Bernadette telephoned, and then she spoke as if she had nothing more in mind than the desire to give a personal thank-you to the old nun for attending her mother's funeral. But when she stood at the door, wrapped in an ankle-length raincoat, its hood pulled forward over her bowed head, Kim had a premonition that this was not a routine visit.

Kim took the coat and pointed down the hall, and by the time she got there Bernadette was standing in front of Emtee Dempsey's desk. "My father did not kill my mother."

"Of course he didn't."

Bernadette slumped into a chair, her bottom lip out of control. By the time Kim got to her and put her arm around her, she was weeping in a way that wrenched the heart. She tried to talk again before getting control of herself, and the words came out separately but their meaning was clear. Bernadette thought her father was trying to protect her.

"He thinks I did it," she said. "He thinks I could have done such a thing."

"Why would he think that?"

"The boots!"

Sister Mary Teresa was preternaturally patient with Bernadette, no doubt confident that what the young woman had to say was well worth the wait. And so it was. The yellow boots found in her father's closet were of the kind Bernie and her husband wore around the golf course in the morning when the dew was heavy. The ground crew wore them until the sun burned off the dew. They made sense. People kidded her about it, but it was better than being sopping wet every day of the season.

"But the boots found in your father's workroom were those of a man."

Bernadette lifted her foot. It was large. Very large. And wide. "Even if they made such boots for women I couldn't get into them. My feet were Daddy's size when I was fourteen years old. It was a family joke. Not to my mother—" She stopped herself with a visible effort.

"Are your boots missing?"

"No."

"No!" The light caught Emtee Dempsey's glasses so that they were opaque disks during the moment when her disappointment might have been visible.

"He bought a pair like mine. He must have. He heard about that print in the bedroom, in the talcum powder, and he assumed it was mine."

"Child, everyone knows you were there. You found the body."

"But I wasn't wearing boots. The police asked me that and I told them. He should have known."

Between the old nun's remark and Bernadette's answer lay a possibility that was not realized. Kim would never overtly think that Emtee Dempsey was willing the girl to say she had been wearing those boots when she discovered her mother's body. No problem then with the boot print; no further need for her father, in a lapse of thinking, to rise to her defense by confessing because he thought the boot print incriminated her. If being in the room incriminated Bernadette, she would have been the prime suspect all along.

Bernadette was still there when Katherine called on the cellular phone in Laura's car.

"We are on our way to see you with important news."

"Good."

"I am speaking to you from a moving automobile using what is called a cellular phone."

"Katherine, long distance calls now go by way of satellite."

"You're impressed and you know it."

The important news was that Laura with a photograph of Gregory Doyle had located a dealer who had sold him a pair of yellow rubber boots, the ones found in the closet of his workroom.

"Two days *after* the murder," Katherine said.

"Thank God!" Bernadette cried.

"Amen," said Emtee Dempsey.

NINETEEN

I WILL MAKE A MOTION to have the indictment dropped." Gregory Doyle nodded.

"The boots the police thought made their case don't. You bought them after the murder."

"Who says so?"

"The clerk who sold them to you."

He thought about that.

"You don't seem very happy. You understand, there's no more reason to say you did it."

"But I did."

"I don't believe you. Are you trying to protect someone?"

"Who?"

"I don't know who. Mr. Doyle, you didn't kill your wife. What kind of guilt are you trying to work out by claiming you did?"

"It's simply retributive justice."

"But what are you making retribution for?"

For the first time Irene Maloney wondered if her client had all his marbles. Their first interview had borne out what Mr. Rush had led her to expect. When he claimed to have killed his wife after the boots were found at his place, she had wavered. My

God, what if he really had done it? Wanting her to plead him guilty was nonsense, but the alternative of pleading him guilty by reason of insanity was hardly attractive. When she learned of the reporter's tracking down the purchase of the boots, a great weight seemed to lift from her. She had not expected this reaction and it angered her.

"All right, you killed your wife. Let's talk about it. What time was it when you killed her?"

"During the night."

"Be specific. When?"

"I can't be. I wandered around for quite a while. Finally I got up my nerve."

"So we don't know what time it was. How did you get to the house? Just wander over?"

"I drove to the neighborhood first."

"And then you started to wander. I am sure one of the neighbors will have seen you. People don't stroll around there in yellow rubber boots for an indefinite period of time without being noticed."

"It was night."

"All the more reason you should have been seen."

"That doesn't follow."

"We'll see. Okay. Finally you stopped wandering and approached the house. How?"

"I went to the back door."

"You came up the driveway and went in the back door."

"I came across the lawn."

"That's right. You wanted to get your boots wet so you could track up the carpet. Mr. Doyle, the great flaw is that you weren't wearing boots."

"I never said I was."

He was right, he hadn't said that. It didn't matter. "Whoever killed your wife was wearing boots."

"Because there were boot prints? That doesn't follow."

"What kind of shoes were you wearing?"

"None. I was barefoot."

"You're just making this up!"

It didn't matter, finally. Anyone can confess to a crime, but it takes evidence and a prosecutor and a judge to hold one accountable, and in the case of Gregory Doyle it was clear the man was lying.

"What's he up to?" the prosecutor, Sirridge, asked Irene.

"I wish I knew."

"Is he wacko?"

"He's one of the sanest, most intelligent men I've ever met."

Sirridge tucked in her chin and looked at Irene over her glasses. "Careful. He's a widower now."

"I'm in love with Benjamin Rush."

"Who isn't?"

So the potential adversaries parted wary friends. Who knew when they would confront one another again. Irene arranged for the two mad professors to see Doyle before he was released. They had been creating a near riot in the jail, insisting they had to see Gregory Doyle. Kotarski was the real nutty one. Stone had moments of clarity.

"What's it about?" Irene asked Stone.

"I can't say."

"Not good enough. Why should I take you in to see him if you won't tell me why? I'm going to be there, and I'll hear everything you say to him."

Stone glanced at Kotarski, who sat with his head thrown back, eyes closed, as if at any moment he would start howling. Irene had not told Stone that her client should be released and on the street within the hour. She was curious about what had caused them to camp here, demanding to see Doyle.

"It's business."

She waited. Stone leaned toward her.

"Your client has in his possession a very valuable book of Professor Kotarski's. Kotarski just heard Doyle is in jail. He wants his property."

"What's the name of the book?"

"Doyle will know. Believe me."

He knew. He would be happy to see Kotarski and Stone. Irene arranged to have the professors brought in. Kotarski came spinning into the room, looking about as if unable to believe his eyes, then claimed a chair across from Doyle.

"I want my manuscript! I demand you return my manuscript."

"I didn't finish it before…" An apologetic smile. "I'm being evicted from here, I'm told. Don't you want me to finish?"

"Where is the manuscript?"

Irene grabbed one of Kotarski's arms and Stone the other and they managed to restrain him. He had lunged toward Doyle as if he meant to spring across the table and throttle the book dealer.

"Don't worry. It's perfectly safe. It is in my vault."

"I want it now."

With Stone's help she got Kotarski out of the visiting room with the promise that Doyle would take him directly to his vault and return the manuscript. Laura Cousins was outside.

"When will he be released?" she asked, but she was distracted by the two professors, only one of whom would Irene now concede was mad. Stone was restraining his colleague and assuring him that he would have his manuscript immediately. "What's that all about?"

"A dissatisfied customer."

She went back in to her client, leaving Laura with the professors. Fifteen minutes later, when she emerged with Doyle, the two professors leapt to their feet. She bundled them all into her car. Doyle was in the passenger seat, Kotarski was moaning in back, Stone was trying to carry on a conversation about some lecture series. It was a relief to pull into Doyle's reserved parking space behind his store.

From his vault, Doyle brought out a box which he carefully opened while Kotarski and Stone hovered over it. After a glance inside, Kotarski threw back his head, but what emerged was not a moan.

"Te Deum laudamus, te dominum confitemur," he sang, in a loud, unsure, but majestic voice. Then he took Doyle's hand and began to cover it with kisses. "I never doubted you, my friend. Never!" He turned and glared at Stone. "This one frightened me to death. Why did you lead me to doubt Mr. Doyle?"

Stone threw up his hands and rolled his eyes.

"I'll be able to finish it now that—" Doyle said.

"No! I must have it with me. I will take it. You understand."

"No, I don't. Unless something is done, it will continue to deteriorate."

Kotarski had closed the box and was clutching it to his breast. He looked to Stone and then to Irene for guidance.

"How valuable is it?" she asked Doyle.

"Very. There is no telling what it would bring at auction. Hundreds of thousands, more. There aren't a lot of thirteenth-century manuscripts on the market."

He told her what Kotarski had asked him to do. It was clear it was a task he wanted to perform. After hugging his possession for a few minutes, Kotarski began to see reason. He put it back on the counter. He took Doyle's hand in both of his.

"Take it back, my friend. Do the necessary restoration work." He turned to Stone. "What is the date of my lecture at the Newberry?"

It was agreed all around that the manuscript would be ready for Kotarski to make a dramatic revelation on the occasion of his lecture. Meantime, not a word. The four of them actually exchanged handshakes for several minutes. It was like being at mass.

The manuscript might have remained a secret if Laura Cousins had not found in the melodrama starring the two professors something to put into her final story on Gregory Doyle's supposed involvement in his former wife's murder.

TWENTY

KATHERINE BROUGHT Laura Cousins with her to Walton Street, confident that her three friends would be delighted to meet her junior colleague, and so they were. It was a treat Katherine had long promised Laura, and she could see the young reporter's incredulous delight as Sister Mary Teresa held forth. She was astonished that Katherine seemed to want to celebrate the resolution of the Margaret Nelson Doyle case.

"But who is the murderer?"

"An intruder she had the misfortune to surprise when he was ransacking the house."

"The house? I understood that only one room was disturbed."

Laura was happy to review the details of the murder with the old nun, and Katherine relaxed with her sherry. Maybe Sister Mary Teresa could not accept an unknown housebreaker as the murderer, but Katherine could. She knew the number of murders that are committed almost by inadvertence, on the spur of the moment, randomly. It is horrible, no doubt about it, the cheapening of life one sees all about one. Children drinking milk at a kitchen table are killed by a stray bullet, a motorist stopped for a light is shot at from a passing car. Such deeds are intended, perhaps, but the victim might have been anyone else. Would Emtee Dempsey ever believe that Margaret had been killed by a stranger for no deeper reason than he did not want her alive to be able to identify him?

"The one room was ransacked yet nothing was taken?"

"The man was interrupted in his work," Katherine said.

"Not so, Katherine. He put the murder weapon on the dresser and apparently wiped the blood off his hands. Am I not right, Laura?"

"You are. And he could have cleaned out her purse. There was a goodly amount in traveler's checks there."

And on and on they went, actually writing out the schedule of events, the estimated time of death, the time of Bernadette O'Brien's discovery of the body, the fact that she was not wearing boots as her father apparently had feared.

"Did she notice the famous boot mark?"

"No. But she didn't notice the statuette on the dresser either. It sounds as if she looked around and got out of there almost immediately when she saw what had happened."

"Sensible woman."

Joyce warmed to the possibility of the killer's being hidden in a closet while Bernadette was in the room, but the old nun waved away such gothic speculation.

"What was he after?" she said. "That is the question."

Kim suggested another possibility. "Nothing was taken because it wasn't a bungled burglary. The man came in order to kill her, and messing up the room was meant to make the police think it had been a robbery."

Emtee Dempsey narrowed her eyes at the suggestion, obviously liking it.

"Has anyone checked to see exactly where the sons were at the time of the murder?"

On her second glass of sherry, Katherine Senski wearied of this obsessive concentration on events that were, so far as she was concerned, over and done with. God rest the soul of Margaret Nelson Doyle and all that, but it did no good to keep raking over facts that had been on the table for days.

"Laura, tell our friends about the mad professors."

"All I know I put into my story."

"Story? What story?"

The newspaper was fetched and Laura asked to read her wrap-up of the case against Gregory Doyle. Her account of the two professors who awaited

Doyle's release after having made nuisances of themselves for hours trying to get to see him provided a nice light note on which to end.

"Kotarski and Stone, mad professors? Nonsense, they are friends of mine."

"You'll have to do better than that, Sister Mary Teresa. Kotarski sounds certifiable to me."

"He is brilliant." But a little smile played on her lips. "Eccentric, yes, as many brilliant people are." She trained an eye on Katherine, daring her to speak. "Laura, what exactly was it they had to see him about?"

"Let me finish my story."

Kotarski had left a valuable book with Doyle and was in a panic lest something had happened to it because of Doyle's arrest.

"They all left for his shop with Irene Maloney when Doyle assured him his property was safe."

"More sherry, Katherine?" Joyce asked, but her tone invited refusal.

Katherine refused. "I don't suppose you have such a thing as a cup of tea?"

Tea sounded good all around, and then minutes later, with Sister Mary Teresa pouring, they sat in the living room, the murder of Margaret Doyle an exhausted topic at last. Laura wanted to know all about the Order of Martha and Mary and how the three of them had ended up on Walton Street.

"It sounds as if it would make a wonderful story."

"My dear, if you write a word about us I will never speak to you again. We cherish our obscurity and have no desire for publicity."

Katherine managed to restrict her reaction to a chuckle.

TWENTY-ONE

"WHY NOT TAKE HIM to dinner at the clubhouse?" Augie asked.

"Am I that bad a cook?"

"Hey." He took her in his arms.

"You going to help me with my swing?"

"Can you afford me?"

Kidding around when they were alone could get quickly serious. Bernie freed herself. "I just think he might prefer a nice private dinner with his daughter and her husband. Think of what he's been through."

"You're the boss."

"Well, this afternoon I don't want to be an employee."

"I'll ask Boris to keep an eye on things in the pro shop."

"An evil eye?"

"Bernie, he's okay."

"I'm kidding." Sort of. Boris hovered about like the angel of judgment.

So Bernie had the afternoon to prepare the lamb chop dinner that was meant to welcome her father back to freedom. And to wonder what they could possibly talk about. For so many years her heart had ached for him, but he wouldn't talk about her mother, admit she was a pain in the neck and was acting like a kid. She wanted to separate and take a fling at business? He professed to find that understandable. Everybody liked to think the travel posters pictured a real world. When you flew off and saw the storied places—well, often they didn't measure up. Meaning he thought she would tire of her discontents and come to see the attractions of the life she had. She might have tired of one dream, but she only replaced it with another. And then the divorce.

"We'll always be married, your mother and I. You know that."

"In the eyes of the Church?"

"In the eyes of God."

He believed that, and he half believed that his wife's discontent was something he had brought about, that if he had been a better husband—well, who knew what she would have been like? But mainly he lived in the expectation that she would come back to him.

"She has to do it, Bernie. Even if I could force her, I wouldn't. That's the spooky thing about marriage, it has to be voluntary on both sides."

Sure it did. Both the man and the woman said "I do," but then the years, habit, familiarity—and love—glued it together in such a way it was unimaginable that it could come apart. This is how she had

seen her parents' marriage, up until the time that
Cece Cord began to hang around and her mother
became embarrassing, asking all those questions
about Cece's father. Her mother came to believe she
could wish herself back beyond the moment when
she had been a trembling bride and what she would
find there would be her real self. Had she ever come
to see how silly that was?

Now she was dead and her father had unsuccessfully tried to be punished for it, confessing to a murder no one imagined he could have committed. With
Augie, she had settled on the explanation that he really did feel guilty because her mother had flaked
out. If things had gone right, if they had stayed together, if he had been in the house with her, she
would be alive today. Augie made a face.

"That's pretty far out."

Of course Augie had always seen her mother as the
guilty party. He didn't know why they should have
anything to do with Margaret, given what she was
doing to her husband, given the effect that had on
Bernie. She supposed she did dwell on it a lot, but
how in heaven's name can you just ignore it when
your mother is going through a teenage phase?

"Why doesn't she move to Hong Kong and do
whatever it is she wants to do there? Why hang
around Chicago where people she ought to care
about have to be witnesses?"

The closest they had ever come to a quarrel was over her mother. Funny, she usually began those sessions, bitching about the latest episode in her mother's sordid career, but when Augie chimed in and upped the ante, suggesting they advise her mother to leave Chicago and quit ruining everybody else's life, Bernie got defensive and they ended up on opposite sides even though they really agreed.

"You're no more responsible for her than Augie would be for me if I made a fool of myself," she told her father.

"Thank God for Augie."

"I do."

"I mean it, Bernie. You are very very lucky to have such a husband."

Well, she was, though how he could know how good Augie was mystified Bernie a bit. Tom had been engaged and broke it off, and Brian just grinned suggestively when asked if and when he meant to marry. Bernie realized what she and Augie might seem like for her father: the one success in a family that was now disintegrating.

"I told him to take back the house and cut her off."

"Augie, you didn't!"

"He's too good for his own good, Bernie. Why should he let her walk all over him? She gets the house, he gets the little apartment. He works his rear end off, she spends the money."

"What did he say?"

"What would Saint Francis say? He patted my arm, smiled, and thanked me."

"Augie, you and I—our marriage means a lot to him."

"Well, it means a helluva lot more to me, and I'm not going to let that woman be a dark cloud over us. I don't care if she is your mother. Having you may be the one good thing she did."

"Oh, I'm a real prize."

"You are!"

"Augie! I have a tendency to slice!"

A moment of astonishment, then he grinned and hugged her to him. She had resolved never to let them talk about her mother again.

THAT NIGHT all they talked about was the medieval manuscript her father was working on for the crazy professor and his friend, whose vigil at the jail before Gregory Doyle had been released had put a comic finish to the whole episode.

"I don't blame him for being nervous. He conned a Polish monastery out of it and stands to become a rich man when he auctions it off."

"How many like it are there?"

Augie's question enabled her father to go on about manuscripts and their transmission. Bernie had heard it before, but he made it sound so exciting it was as if the story were new. Printed editions of classics depended on all those centuries when hand-copied versions of the texts were passed on from generation to generation.

"There is something like twelve hundred years between Plato and our oldest manuscript of one of his writings. We have to assume that all those centuries were bridged by now-lost copies from which our oldest manuscript derives."

Either Augie was really interested or he was putting on a good act, but he prompted her father with questions, allowing him to dominate the table talk, if so mild-mannered a man could be said to dominate anything.

"Thanks," she said to Augie, when they stood watching her father go down the drive.

"He's like a new man."

THE NEXT MORNING when Augie was out playing an instructional round with a member, Boris came into the pro shop from the workroom in back carrying a pair of boots. He displayed them like a fisherman's catch.

"Someone put these under the workbench."

"I'll take them."

"Yours?"

She nodded, trying not to stare at the boots.

"When I turned on the space heater, these began to spread their perfume."

Bernie took them and put them in the trash barrel outside. For the next hour, she tried to forget them. Her boots were in the apartment. No one from the ground crew would have been in the workshop. Later, when she went to check the mail, she fished the boots out of the barrel and took them along. *AO* was written with a Magic Marker inside the right boot.

TWENTY-TWO

GEOFFREY STONE HAD approached Kotarski in the dual role of supplicant and patron; now he had become the eccentric scholar's baby-sitter. Kotarski had been a trembling neurotic ever since he learned that the man to whom he had entrusted the most valuable possession he was ever likely to have was in jail, accused of murder, indeed a self-confessed murderer. Coherence fled and he had been a babbling mess all the way downtown on what Stone assumed was a pointless journey, but even when, after a delay, they had indeed been shown in to see Gregory Doyle, even after they had all adjourned to Doyle's shop where Kotarski had been assured that his precious manuscript had been as locked up as Doyle himself, his ward was like a child who for the first time realizes that the great globe itself spins without support in space.

"I would have killed myself," Kotarski said, emptying his glass. He was clearly determined to kill the bottle they had left in order to seek out Doyle.

"Life is more important than a manuscript."

Kotarski just looked at him, but then Stone had not spoken with complete sincerity. He would not of course have traded Kotarski for a piece of skin on which a thirteenth-century scribe had written and which had managed to survive into the twentieth century, but there was little doubt as to their relative market value.

Kotarski had flicked on his microfilm reader as soon as they returned from Doyle's and now sat with his head under its cowl-like hood, studying the facsimile of his manuscript. That film ensured that the contents of his find would not be lost, but it was the manuscript as artifact that was the true discovery. The work on agriculture it contained was already known through other copies. How could a picture compare with the feel of a manuscript on which another human hand had written seven hundred years ago?

"You and Sister Mary Teresa will be the stars of my lecture series."

"What will she speak on?" Kotarski's head emerged and his eyes gleamed with paranoia.

"Have you met her?"

"Years ago."

"As a courtesy, I think we should call on her so that you can give her a preview of your finding."

Kotarski liked the role Stone was casting him for. He began to nod.

"Perhaps we should wait until Doyle has finished with the manuscript."

"Shall we let her decide?"

Sister Mary Teresa was delighted by the prospect of a visit from the distinguished scholar Joseph Kotarski ("Her very words," Stone assured him). What scholar has ever received the recognition he considers his due? Sister Mary Teresa's quite obviously sincere eagerness to receive them would have overcome any reluctance Kotarski might feel. They arranged to meet the following morning in the house on Walton Street.

"Meanwhile, we can finish this whishkey."

ON THE FOLLOWING DAY, Stone had a head like a balloon when he mounted the steps to the front door of the house on Walton Street, a bright-eyed and voluble Kotarski at his side. How could the man be so cheerful after the amount of whiskey he had poured down that giraffelike throat of his the night before? When the first bottle was empty, Kotarski had brought out another. Well, how often does one celebrate the allaying of such a fear as had gripped him when he heard of Doyle's arrest?

At the nun's suggestion they had brought the microfilm with them, and within minutes of their arrival she was examining it through a considerably better viewer than Kotarski's.

"I congratulate you, Professor. How did you ever come into possession of such a treasure?"

He gave the old nun a much longer version of its provenance, the Franciscan community that had thrived in Poland under an adverse regime, the walls bursting with vocations and, now, with freedom, feeling the pinch of poverty. His cousin, a friar in the community, had consulted Kotarski and been over-joyed to receive the modest amount the professor could offer for the manuscript. The old nun's brows rose in silent moral comment.

"If this manuscript brings as much at auction as I hope, I shall act as agent for the community in the sale of other things."

"Perhaps you would give Professor Kotarski a preview of your lecture, Sister Mary Teresa."

"It is nothing as exciting as this, needless to say. You will eclipse us all, Professor."

Kotarski showed his yellow smile. The three of them spent an enjoyable hour, informing one an-other of ongoing research, telling battle stories of the academic and scholarly life, three veterans finding in retrospect the keenest joy of all. Stone deflected the suggestion of sherry and was relieved to see Kotar-ski pouring coffee rather than alcohol down his un-slakable throat. He put Kotarski into a cab at the corner, and the proud scholar flourished the box of microfilm before folding himself into the back seat. His nicotine-stained teeth showed in a farewell smile as he was driven away.

At the time, all Stone felt was relief finally to have gotten rid of the pain in the neck. No doubt he was a great scholar and his lecture would be the jewel of the series because of his great luck in getting hold of that damned manuscript, but seeing him on two consecutive days was too much of a good thing.

He saw him the following day as well, on the front page of the *Tribune*. Over a photograph of the dead body of Joseph Kotarski was the headline, *PROFESSOR SLAIN IN HOME.*

TWENTY-THREE

EMTEE DEMPSEY READ the news in silence, made no comment after putting down the paper, and went silently to her study, where half an hour later she still sat motionless at her desk, staring straight ahead. Kim's presence penetrated her concentration and she looked at her.

"Yes, my dear?"

"Are you all right?"

"Yes. Thank you."

"Don't want to talk?"

"Come and sit down."

Kim sat across the desk and waited for the old nun to speak. It wasn't right that she should say nothing at all about this.

"That's twice."

"Twice."

"First Margaret, now Professor Kotarski."

Kim felt a great relief at the implication of the statement. Poor Professor Kotarski was the victim of a burglary, and the same had been true of Margaret Doyle. The great difference was that the thief had known what he wanted when he broke into Professor Kotarski's. Emtee Dempsey's silence was due to

her reluctant acceptance of the fact that there were
no culprits in either case, at least none who had any
connection with the victim. Professor Kotarski, like
Margaret Doyle, had been a threatening nuisance to
eliminate in the course of a break-in. As a historian,
the old nun could have given an impromptu lecture
on the illogical connection between events and their
antecedents; in history things just happen that so
easily might not have come about if some totally un-
predictable and unrelated thing had not first occurred. The fortuitous nature of things was something she found difficult to accept when they came
close to home, however. Like the police, she had assumed that if Margaret had been killed, an explanation for this could be found in what had gone before,
an explanation that would involve those Margaret
knew. To accept her death as random was not easy.
To accept the murder of Professor Kotarski as
equally random and irrational had reduced her to silence.

"It would of course be folly to blame Katherine's
young friend for alerting every thief in the city to the
professor's great treasure."

"Did the murderer think he kept such a thing in
his apartment?"

"And why wouldn't he? Where had Kotarski kept
it before he turned it over to Mr. Doyle for restora-

tion? Where would it have been if he had gone through on his threat to take it from Doyle's vault?''

The phone began to ring, of course, first Professor Stone, to whom Emtee Dempsey spoke for half an hour in soothing tones, assuring the distraught scholar that he had nothing to blame himself for. Stone too linked what had happened with the scene he and Kotarski had put on downtown, trying to get in to see Doyle. Katherine Senski called to say she was on her way to the house. Before lunch, to which Richard was invited, they knew all there was to know—that is, all that the press and police knew—of what had happened to Professor Joseph Kotarski.

He had been found fully clothed, presumably because he had fallen asleep while drinking and then wakened to find a thief prowling his apartment. Stone described Kotarski as engaged in an almost continuous bibulous celebration since securing the manuscript for a pittance from his impoverished Polish relative, but drunk or sober the ill-built Kotarski would have been no match for a determined burglar. If the professor's apartment had always been the mess Stone claimed it was, it had nonetheless been torn pretty thoroughly apart by the one who had broken in and then struck down the aroused tenant. The murder weapon was a block of plastic in which was embedded a medallion bearing the coat of arms of Kotarski's university. The microfilm reader had been toppled and papers and books spilled everywhere, reels of microfilm snaking between the workroom and the living room in which the body had been found.

"Was anything missing?"

Richard shrugged. "Apparently not, but I can't say for sure. Stone has agreed to look over the rooms to see if anything obvious is gone."

"A thief who took nothing would be an odd thief."

Richard disagreed, and of course he had stories. The number of bungled burglaries could make one believe that the Three Stooges were loose in Chicago. The common note was speed. Even an inept burglar was in and out of a place in minutes. In that time he had to find something negotiable and portable.

"They don't hang around if they don't strike oil immediately."

"Like what?" Emtee Dempsey asked.

"These are addicts. They need something they can sell and sell fast: electronic equipment, televisions, VCRs, stereos, CD players, cameras."

"Didn't Professor Kotarski have a microfilm reader?"

"If that's the huge metal thing that was knocked off a table, he had one. Past tense. The screen broke when it hit the floor."

"Didn't anyone hear anything?"

"His apartment is on the first floor."

"Would such a thief know what to do with a medieval manuscript if he had one?"

Richard took this to be a suggestion that there was no connection between the break-in and the killing and Kotarski's unwitting announcement to the city that he had come into possession of an invaluable thirteenth-century manuscript. This was too much for Emtee Dempsey.

"No, Richard. We must resolutely adhere to the view that he was killed because of that manuscript."

"We? Don't tell me you plan to involve yourself in our investigation? I am telling you these things in order to prevent just that. Besides, our investigation is over with. Callous as it sounds, this is just another routine murder as far as I'm concerned."

"It's a wonder anyone feels safe in his bed, Richard."

"Maybe if Kotarski had gone to bed he would have slept through the whole thing and been alive today."

Such philosophizing was not to Sister Mary Teresa's taste. "Maybe if he had not put it into the mind of some poor desperate addict that a priceless treasure was to be had for the taking, he would be alive today."

"Yeah. And maybe if I left here right now I could be in my office in fifteen minutes."

In the hallway, when Kim was showing him out, Richard turned to her. "Distract her, Kim. Keep her out of this. Take her to the lake for a few days."

"So she won't interfere?"

"So she won't interfere."

"I thought your investigation was closed."

"It is. And I want it to stay that way."

She watched him bounce down the steps and cross the walk to his car, unmarked but boldly sitting in a NO PARKING place. Her big brother. She loved him, she admired him, but she found herself siding with Emtee Dempsey. It didn't seem right that a nice old man like Professor Kotarski should have no more distinctive epitaph than that he happened to be killed by a thief. By all rights, the man should have died from smoking all those cigarettes.

TWENTY-FOUR

THE DREADFUL and pointless attack on Kotarski filled Gregory Doyle with a feeling that had grown more and more familiar to him over the years: the wish that he did not live in the present age. The past with its artifacts attracted, just as the deeds of all the dead, being done, took on a kind of narrative sense that current happenings could not have. The present moment represented chaos and absurdity, the past the serenity of what for good or ill was over and done and need now only be contemplated.

The feeling had given him an affinity with Kotarski; he had sensed that as they talked. The antic professor had come to him, eyes aglow, whispering in a way that would have delighted a director coaching an actor in audible asides, screwing his face into an expression of shrewdness. Doyle recognized him as a completely impractical man. The only value Joseph Kotarski would derive from his study of the past would fit nearly between his two ears. Did he even really want anything more? Doyle would have wagered that, in the end, after auctioning the manuscript, Kotarski would have sent the profits to his cousin's Franciscan house near Cracow.

"I have spoken to Sister Mary Teresa," Stone said. They sat in Doyle's workroom behind his shop among the smells of leather and glue and ink.

"Kotarski knew her?"

"He had met her. I reintroduced them to one another only yesterday. I took him to the convent. He was a Catholic, of course. More or less."

"Most of us Catholics are less than we should be."

Kotarski had been unable not to make comparisons between the house on Walton Street and the impoverished community in which his cousin lived.

"She said to him how pleased his cousin must be. Kotarski was nonplussed. She explained. His cousin is a Franciscan for whom poverty is a choice, not a disaster."

Doyle thought of the house on Walton Street. Despite its architectural interest, not many Chicagoans who had homes at all would prefer living there, following the routine of the nuns. Nuns too seemed engaged in the effort to live in some century other than the present, though the one time he had suggested this to Sister Mary Teresa, she shook her great headdress vigorously.

"Have you ever heard of the grace of the present moment, Mr. Doyle?"

If he hadn't before, he heard of it then. When other than now can we do the deeds that decide our eternal condition? She went on to speak of Kierke-

gaard's discussion of the "contemporary of Christ."
All in all, as always, he got far more than he bar-
gained for in talking with her. He loved the old nun.
He loved her more than Margaret ever had, yet he
knew it was only because he had married Margaret
that he had entrée to the house on Walton Street.
Benjamin Rush had underwritten very interesting
and rewarding searches for books on behalf of Sister Mary Teresa, and she had recommended him because she had learned that he was Margaret's
husband. Separated husband. Divorced husband. He
had never been able to think of himself as her former husband. He would always be Catholic enough
to know that the vows they had exchanged years ago
were good for life, no matter what either of them
later did. Once or twice he had toyed with the idea of
taking Shirley Loudon to dinner, but he would have
felt foolish asking her. Lavinia, giggling, had told
him she was going out on a date with her friend Virgie and her boyfriend Billy.

"Just the three of you?"

"Oh, they got a man for me."

"What does Virgie do?"

"Oh, she cleans house like I do. Billy now, he's
something else. That man always got money, always
ready for a good time."

Lavinia's foolish grin made her seem a sister of poor Margaret, middle-aged yet still stirred by the prospect of romantic adventure.

"He showed Sister Mary Teresa a microfilm of the manuscript," Stone said.

The manuscript itself was still safe in Doyle's vault. It was conceivable that someone could get into that vault, but it would take the prowess of a bank robber, not the furtive skills of a petty thief.

"Were you aware that a reporter was there when you talked about the manuscript before they let him in to see me?"

"Kotarski couldn't keep quiet about it. I tried to shut him up. He was drunk, you know."

The sour smell of whiskey had been more than evident when Kotarski lunged at him in the visiting room at the jail. What did he imagine had happened to his manuscript? Even sober, Kotarski's mind went along paths difficult to follow.

"I don't think he ever expressed any concern about the security of the manuscript. His worry was that someone might steal his thunder in announcing the discovery. Before he brought it to me, he kept it in that rat's nest of his."

"The thief must have assumed it was there last night."

"I wonder if he knew what he was looking for?"

Lavinia, the cleaning woman, had been fussing around in the room as they talked. She had an impressionistic notion at best of what the room should look like after her labors. Doyle preferred her to work in the store, where the tasks were simple: straighten and dust the books on the shelf, mop the floors, vacuum, do the front window. He had inherited her from the house, one of the shared spoils of the divorce settlement. Margaret was no happier with Lavinia's work than he was but used the curious argument that scolding her might lead her to quit. Gregory would have thought that was the idea.

"Where would we find another cleaning woman?"

"Another?"

Nonetheless he had her come to the store one day a week and make a pest of herself under the guise of cleaning. She loved the smells of the workshop, as well perhaps as the impossibility of his telling afterward what if anything she had done, and spent as much time there as she could.

His question caused Stone to stand and bring his chair closer. This got him out of the way of Lavinia's dust mop and heralded his confidential tone.

"You've put your finger on it. How may people in Chicago would understand the value of Kotarski's find? How many would recognize it if it were under their nose? How many would know what to do with it if they did take it and wanted to realize a profit from it?''

"The kind of person you are describing might want simply to have it.''

"In any case, it is a small number of people. Kotarski and I go way back, most of us do. We make a small invidious band, fiercely loyal, fiercely jealous of one another. A short list could contain all competent Chicago paleographers.''

"Would Sister Mary Teresa be on it?''

"Oh, no, no. Of course not. She is a historian. True, she sometimes deals with manuscripts, but her reliance is at second hand. She must depend on philologists, paleographers, codicologists. I do not say this in criticism,'' he added, as if aware of his own tone of voice. "She is an eminent historian.''

"Do you and she go way back?''

"Not at all! Our acquaintance is quite new. You see, we do not till the same fields.''

Of course Doyle's work brought him into contact with scholars like Stone and Kotarski, and he would know a good number of those who would figure on Stone's imaginary list of Chicago paleographers.

"Don't forget graduate students, Professor. How many students of history, philosophy, literature, music, acquire some manuscript training? Enough to date the scribe's hand, guess at the provenance of the manuscript?''

"True." Stone did not sound as if he really believed it. "But greed is an old man's vice. The young are idealists, altruists, not yet possessive. They quite naturally think of such treasures as in the public domain, the property of everyone."

"Have you said this to Sister Mary Teresa?"

"What on earth for?"

Stone had said he did not know the old nun well. Perhaps Doyle would not have been as familiar with Emtee Dempsey's extracurricular activities if he had not married Margaret, but he had found it impossible not to notice the way in which she seemed to involve herself in any difficulties involving her old students. No doubt on most alumnae she had a benign influence that kept them from the possibility of trouble, but any graduate of the College of Martha and Mary who got into difficulties, let alone fell afoul of the law, could count on the old nun's solidarity and support. Doyle had been a beneficiary of that himself, again because of Margaret. Sister Mary Teresa had sent Benjamin Rush to him, and he in turn arranged for Irene Maloney to represent him. Irene at least must surely regret having become involved with him.

That morning he had telephoned her and insisted that she send the bill for her services to him.

"That is not my decision."

"Whose? Benjamin Rush's?"

"Mr. Rush doesn't involve himself in the day-to-day details of the firm."

"Irene, I insist on paying."

"Very well. You may take me to lunch."

Lunch was a meal Gregory Doyle had long since learned to forgo. It took valuable time from the middle of the day; it added unnecessary calories to his intake; it was depressingly habit-forming. In his lunch-going days he had often spent a portion of the morning deciding whom to have lunch with. But lunch entailed closing the shop, and the lunch hour was often when customers popped in. He did not want to lose the business; even more he regretted time lost in his workroom in back. It was, then, something of a sacrifice to agree to take Irene to lunch. They arranged to meet at the Doyenne at twelve-thirty, and now, while he talked with Stone, Doyle was conscious of his coming luncheon engagement.

TWENTY-FIVE

THE EIGHTH HOLE at Meadowbrook had been changed from a 4 to a 3 par by bringing the tee thirty yards closer to the green. From being an easy 4, it became a difficult 3. Bernadette cranked into her swing, bringing the club head back with the precision of Nancy Lopez and then coming through, shifting her weight, keeping her upper arms close to her body, never taking her eyes from the ball. By the time she deigned to look up, her ball was describing a beautiful trajectory, fading into the green and coming to a stop ten feet above the hole.

"Damn," Bernadette said, stopping to pick up her tee.

"What's wrong with that?" asked Mrs. Wiggles.

"I'll have a downhill putt."

Any pleasure she had felt with her own shot went as she watched Mrs. Wiggles address her ball. She made encouraging suggestions, these were taken, silence fell. On a branch above, a cardinal sang; out on the fairway a gopher scampered from one hole to another; the sound of kids in the pool drifted to them. Mrs. Wiggles stood frozen over her ball. Suddenly, her club whipped back, she slapped at her ball with it, emitting a loud grunt, and ball, tee, and a clump of dirt traveled twenty yards in the direction of the hole. Mrs. Wiggles burst into tears.

It was Mrs. Wiggles's ambition to outplay her nemesis Mrs. Waddles, and these early morning lessons were meant to hone her skills to that end. Bernadette had found it impossible to erase from the woman's mind and bodily memory everything she thought she knew of the game of golf. If they could approach it as a vast unknown continent, things might be different. Alas, it was Mrs. Wiggles's conviction that she was already a golfer, but that somehow her game had fallen on evil days. The 130 to 140 strokes she took on a round had nothing to do with her real game. Such scores represented an anomaly, a temporary trough in her career, and these lessons from Bernadette were meant to restore her to her alleged former prowess so that she could whip the panties off of Edith Waddles.

"She cheats," Mrs. Wiggles said, widening her eyes.

"At golf?"

"I see your point. She cheats at cards too. I shall want witnesses when we play our match, someone to keep an eye on her."

Inherited wealth, the earned money of their husbands, seldom a personally acquired affluence, filled the golf clubs of the nation with the Mrs. Wiggleses

and Mrs. Waddleses with whom it was Bernadette's
fate to deal. Augie had his share of hopeless male
golfers, but they exhibited an awed diffidence before the excellence of his game. They understood
what it was to do something well. But Mrs. Wiggles
and Mrs. Waddles played golf as they played bridge.
They did not so much want to do it well as to do it
better than some foe. Who was it who had called men
rather than women the competitive sex?

Of late, however, Bernadette had thanked God for
the distraction of her clients. On the course, on the
practice range or greens, busy behind the counter of
the pro·shop, she could drive from her mind that pair
of boots Boris had found in the room behind the
shop where clubs were cleaned and repaired. It was
a snug room, a refuge on a rainy day or early in the
season before the rush began, where one could bur-
nish club heads on the motor-driven brushes and
wheels.

Bernadette had not entered the room since the day
Boris had emerged holding Augie's boots and wondering who had hidden them under the bench by the
space heater. She had put them in a plastic bag and
closed it with a twist of wire and hidden them in the
trunk of the car. She might just as well have put them
on the mantel or hung them over the table on which
they ate. She could not forget them. She could not
ignore the significance of their being hidden under

the bench. And even if she could have, her father's first visit since his release would have brought it all back.

"Why did you say you did it?" Augie asked him, frowning and grinning at once.

"A moment of madness."

Bernadette laughed as if it were the joke of the half century. At least Augie could have waited until Boris was out of the shop. Boris, in his early thirties, had the profile of an anteater. His uncut, unwashed hair was slicked back on his head and ended in indecisive curls at the nape of his neck. He looked out at the world with resentment and envy. It was his second year at Meadowbrook, and he gave Bernadette the willies.

"He acts as if he's the rightful heir to the Transylvanian throne."

"He flunked out of college."

"Barber college?"

"Bernie, he's brilliant."

"I know. He told me."

Boris had a two-room apartment in the attic of the clubhouse, its dormer windows providing him a beautiful view to resent. His dour presence keeping things spic and span was a reminder of class warfare. Boris hated them all, their money, their leisure, their clothes, their looks. Once she had let him develop his view that, contrary to what seemed log-

ical, good looks are a function of income. Bernadette kidded him about baths and razors and
shampoo, all accessible to the downtrodden, but
Boris had lost any sense of humor he might have had
when he was booted out of barber college.

"He wants a Ph.D."

An odd ambition. The menial tasks Boris performed at Meadowbrook seemed to match any talents Bernadette could see in him. He did read a lot.

"Books in his own language," Augie said.

"What's that?"

"Not English."

Bernadette didn't like Boris within earshot when
her father was there. Members must know of the
death of her mother, though few said anything to
her. Of course Boris knew, although even his manner had altered when her father was arrested and then
actually confessed. The newspaper had made all that
seem somehow all right after he was released.
"Quixotic" was the term used to express what he had
done. What would her father have said if he had answered Augie honestly when asked why he had confessed to murdering his wife?

Her father must have thought she had made the
boot mark the police had found in the spilled talcum powder in her mother's bedroom. Finally he
realized how crazy that was. If he thought she had
been wearing boots, then there was no mystery about

the boot print. She had found the body. That was one of the first things the police had asked her, what she was wearing on her feet when she went to the house that morning. She hadn't known about the boot print then and thought it a funny thing to be asked, but the earliest newspaper accounts had made it clear it was the killer who had worn the boots and made that imprint in the spilled talcum powder.

Only after Boris found Augie's boots hidden in the back room did she understand what her father had understood from the beginning.

"Gimme?" Mrs. Wiggles asked, looking up. Her ball was six feet from the hole. She had been about to putt for minutes.

"Sure."

Mrs. Wiggles tapped her ball and it dropped into the cup. Her mouth fell open.

"See what you can do when you try?"

TWENTY-SIX

"WHO KNOWS THAT the manuscript is in your care?" Emtee Dempsey asked Mr. Doyle.

"Geoffrey Stone, of course. And anyone else Kotarski might have told."

"But did he tell others?"

"Sister, he was absolutely elated with what he had obtained. Who can blame him? He babbled about it endlessly. On the other hand, he was determined to make a big splash with the announcement of his discovery."

"He had to tell Stone. The revelation was to have been part of a lecture series Professor Stone has arranged at the Newberry Library."

"What's your point, Sister?"

"One theory of the murder of Professor Kotarski is that he was the victim of a break-in. The thief wakened Kotarski and in a panic killed him."

"As with Margaret?"

The great headdress bobbed. "So it seems. But in the case of Professor Kotarski, there is the far more plausible explanation that his killer read of the great discovery, went there to take it, and in the process killed the poor man. For panic at being discovered we can substitute rage at not finding what he had come for.''

''The treasure is safe, Sister. It's in my vault.''

''Where neither moth nor rust consume, nor thief breaks in to steal?''

''It's as safe as it would be anywhere.''

''I think you should take great care, Mr. Doyle. Imagine how that thief must feel, to have killed for nothing. Any chance to get what he had hoped to get by breaking into Kotarski's would seem a risk worth taking.''

Gregory Doyle nodded, but Kim had the feeling that he was humoring Emtee Dempsey. She had felt much the same way when she attended the man's funeral, a melancholy affair at Holy Family Cathedral. Sister Mary Teresa had suggested to her good friend Monsignor Yawl that Kotarski must have a Catholic funeral.

''What was his parish?''

She gave him the address somewhat impatiently. After all, he could have known it from reading the newspaper account of the finding of Kotarski's body. Monsignor Yawl called back to say that the Professor had not been registered in the parish whose territory included his residence.

''He struck me as a man who would attend mass where he wished.''

''You're sure he was a Catholic?''

"Kotarski?"

"Is the Pope Polish?" Monsignor Yawl grinned. There was a gap between his two upper teeth that took ten years from his age and more from his monsignorial dignity.

"His cousin is a Franciscan."

Monsignor Yawl agreed to contact the funeral director who had taken charge of the body. The police had assumed that Kotarski was Jewish and the funeral director had no experience of Catholic funerals, let alone of monsignors with gap teeth. In the end he had gladly relinquished the body to a firm known to the cathedral staff. They had prayed for the man's soul in the chapel of the house on Walton Street, but only Kim had attended the funeral mass. There were half a dozen others in the cathedral, only one to attend the funeral. She was Kotarski's landlady, a wizened lady in a black cloth coat and a babushka. Kim was impressed by her loyalty. She came forward when the funeral director stood at the open door of his limousine, looking hopefully about. Only Kim and the old lady got in.

"You a relative?"

"No. Are you?"

"He lived with me. In my house. A boarder."

"I'm Sister Kimberly."

The woman looked at her outstretched hand for a moment before taking it. "Salvation Army?"

"I am a nun."

"He owes me rent."

Kim told the woman she was sure that all the Professor's debts would be paid.

"But when? I never had a boarder murdered before."

"Thank God for that."

She made a kind of sign of the cross. "Who's paying for all this?"

At the cemetery, Professor Stone got out of his car and came across the lawn to the graveside. The landlady attached herself to him as to a more promising source of Kotarski's rent. Monsignor Yawl could be forgiven for the routine way in which he hurried through the rite of burial. He was used to performing for an audience, and the burial of Joseph Kotarski seemed of interest only to God.

"I'll drive you to Walton Street," Stone offered after Monsignor Yawl was done. Well, nearly. The landlady was now confronting him. Kim felt as if she were deserting him when she slipped into Stone's car and they pulled away.

"Who will pay his landlady?"

Stone made an angry noise. "I doubt she's owed anything. Can you imagine, coming to the funeral in the hope of collecting rent?"

Kim wanted to ask where Kotarski's colleagues were, his friends. In the circumstances, Stone's loyalty stood out. Not even Gregory Doyle had come. But then he had only recently buried his wife and would not have relished a reminder of that. Besides, Kotarski was someone he had done business with, not a friend. Nonetheless, Kim developed a warm feeling for Professor Stone and asked him in when they got to Walton Street. Emtee Dempsey would want to hear about the funeral, and Professor Stone could tell the old nun anything she forgot.

"I didn't go into the church," Stone said defensively. "Things Catholic and Christian are familiar to me in my studies, of course, but I've never been inside a Catholic church."

"Well, how many Catholics have been in synagogues?"

"I'm not Jewish. Funny you should think so. But then I thought Kotarski was."

Emtee Dempsey derived wry amusement from the story about Kotarski's landlady.

"Who will look after his things?"

"The police have sealed his rooms."

"I meant eventually. There will be a lifetime of research there and not everyone would be able to appraise it."

Sister Mary Teresa's papers were destined for the archives at the University of Notre Dame, an arrangement she had made after a series of pilgrimages to Walton Street on the part of a very persuasive archivist. The old nun had been assured that the Dempsey Papers would be quickly cataloged and made available to scholars. The decision had been simple realism. The old nun did not have a valetudinarian bone in her body. She was ready to go at any moment yet lived as if she had decades to go before she slept. Her question brought a gloomy look to Professor Stone, who held his glass of sherry in both hands.

"I don't think he'd made arrangements."

"How old was he?"

"Pushing seventy, I suppose."

"Even so, he should have thought ahead."

The thought that the approach of a seventieth birthday seemed relative youth to his hostess brightened Stone, along with the sherry. He was in his fifties.

"I hope he made a will."

Emtee Dempsey thought she might ask Benjamin Rush to keep an eye on the disposition of Professor Kotarski's estate. The thirteenth-century manuscript would doubtless be the item of greatest monetary value.

"I'm sure he'd want the proceeds of its sale to go to his cousin's monastery in Poland."

"Where else?" Stone said. His lips were sticky with sherry, and he nodded eagerly when Kim suggested a drop more.

Kim sensed in the old nun's questions the desire to prevent Professor Kotarski's death from just sinking into the numberless natural and violent deaths that marked the terminal point of human lives. Of course she did not expect all of them to make sense to her, but Professor Kotarski's path had crossed hers in the final phase of his life and she felt obliged to find some sense in the way it had ended. Prompted by Richard, Kim drew the old nun's attention to the dozens of violent deaths that had taken place in recent weeks in Chicago, the victims and their assailants unknown to one another prior to the fateful meeting when murder had been committed for a pittance.

"I quite see his point."

"He claimed you wouldn't."

"I didn't say I agree."

Nor had she forgotten Margaret Nelson Doyle. The first of a series of masses for the purpose of the soul of her former student was said at the cathedral. And she asked Kim to telephone Bernadette O'Brien and see how she was doing. The result was that Kim and Joyce were invited to play tennis at Meadowbrook.

TWENTY-SEVEN

SHIRLEY LOUDON'S knowledge of the aftermath of Margaret Doyle's murder was not confined to what she read in the newspapers. Meeting Katherine Senski at the house on Walton Street in undoubtedly embarrassing circumstances had been an unlooked-for bonus. Besides, she sensed that the reporter admired the ingenuity of that single wedding invitation even if it had caused her some embarrassment. So Shirley had kept in touch.

"I thought of joining the order," she confided to Katherine.

"If you had, who would have thought you'd be boarding the *Titanic?*"

"Will the order last?"

Katherine was stirring her tea vigorously. Around them in Marshall Field's were representatives of a kind of woman who, if one believed ideologues, was becoming extinct: the shopping matron. Shirley had none of the successful career woman's disdain for the wives and mothers who, like her own mother, made their homes the center of their lives. She did not have it in her to envy the nuns on Walton Street, but it was

very easy to wish her destiny had included a husband and children. Now it was too late for children.

"Last? You should get Sister Mary Teresa going
on that sometime. The question suggests that unless
more years, decades, how long, are added to the history of the order, it was a failure. But is it meant to
endure forever? Probably not. Orders and congre-
gations come and go. Not the major ones perhaps,
Dominicans, Benedictines, Franciscans, but the little ones. They arise to meet some need and, when
times change, their mission is completed. Sister will
do everything she can to make the order survive, but
if it doesn't she will not consider it to have been a
failure."

"Closing the college must have been a blow."

"We fought it tooth and nail. But we were up
against principalities and powers." Katherine
frowned over the tearoom, but she was thinking of
past battles.

"Did you ever consider joining the order?"

The question shocked Katherine. Had she set out
to be what she was, an unmarried professional
woman, doyenne of Chicago reporters? Katherine
wore rings but none of them was a wedding ring.
Shirley had come to admire Katherine, but the old
woman was a warning too. She might already have
passed the point of no return so that she was doomed

to remain unmarried, but Shirley intended to defy her apparent fate.

"I'm just kidding, Katherine. On another subject, why do you think Gregory Doyle confessed to killing his wife?"

"I don't know. Thank God, that's over with."

Katherine was now full of the story of Professor Kotarski, but this was all right with Shirley. That story involved Gregory too. Katherine was proud of the way her protégée Laura Cousins had used the comic scene of the two professors trying to visit Gregory just before he was released from jail. It suggested the unseriousness of his arrest and it pointed to the way he made his living.

Before Margaret left home, Shirley had persuaded Willie in the rare books department of the university library to let her take a sixteenth-century book printed in Florence to Gregory Doyle for restoration.

"I never heard of him," Willie said wetly.

"Does the name Mary Teresa Dempsey mean anything to you?"

Willie rolled his eyes. "She treats this place as if it were a public library."

"She speaks very highly of Doyle."

"Is he bonded?"

"I'll check."

He was, and Willie accepted that they had made an agreement. Shirley felt vulnerable driving through the area around the university with that precious cargo, but she got to Gregory's shop without incident.

It had become familiar to her during these past years when Margaret had been acting so strangely. Shirley had fought the notion that Margaret had stolen the life meant for herself in appropriating Gregory all those years ago. It was difficult to imagine having children of the ages Margaret's were. What had always been easy to imagine was a life with Gregory. That was what had made Margaret's chatter so incredible. At first she had thought it was a conscious teasing, speaking disdainfully of her life with Gregory when she must have known how marvelous it seemed to Shirley.

"Freedom means nothing to you, Shirl, because you've always had it."

"And yours is the life of a slave?"

"Most of it is psychological. The feeling of being tied down, not in control of my own life, unable just to go somewhere if I should want to."

"Where do you want to go?"

Margaret's expression was impatient. "It doesn't matter where. Anywhere."

When they were roommates in college and talked of what life might hold in store for them they had been in search of a point for their lives, a purpose, something in which to lose themselves. It was what, however momentarily, had attracted Shirley to the religious life. To immerse herself in something larger, to see her life as dedicated to a transcendent ideal, to escape the self, that was the attraction. It seemed the definition of love. Hadn't Margaret wanted to disappear into her love for Gregory, and vice versa, two become one? A crooked little smile appeared on Margaret's face when Shirley got some version of this into words.

"Girl talk. I remember those nights." She shook her head. "How young we were."

Margaret seemed younger now than she ever had in college. Then Shirley had regarded her as someone mature and confident, her aim in life clear. What had enabled her to accept Margaret's love for Gregory, and to fight the temptation to think she had stolen him from her, was precisely the beauty of the love they had for one another. How could she begrudge her best friend that?

"If you lived by yourself for a while you'd get over this."

"You mean an experiment?"

Shirley was astounded that Margaret thought she was suggesting such a separation, but Margaret embraced it as if it were an inspiration. Shirley found herself acting as the devil's advocate, finding a dread fascination in the thought of the breakup of Margaret's marriage to Gregory. She had accompanied Margaret when she looked for an apartment. She began to feel like an accomplice. And it gave her an excuse to talk with Gregory.

"I can't believe she's serious, Greg."

"We've reached a dangerous age."

We. Did he include her as well? But what age isn't dangerous?

"I suppose you're going to tell me you've thought of leaving her?"

"I am married to my work. Hasn't she told you?"

"I've brought a book from the rare book room of the library."

He took it as a veterinarian might accept a sick animal, turning it in his hands, his perfect brows lifting in concern. He was more handsome now than when they had first met; the gray in his hair, the network of fine lines on his face, enhanced rather than detracted from his appearance. She studied him as he studied the book.

"This leather could be brought back, but it will take time." He showed her a palm in which the book's binding had left a leathery dust.

"Can you do it?"

"Yes."

"I'll need a receipt." Willie had been very reluctant to let the book leave the library.

"Of course. I am insured. And I'll keep it in my vault."

"Tell me about the process."

And he did, thoroughly, encouraged by her attentiveness, her understanding nods. She scarcely attended to the meaning of the words, preferring to listen to the masculine music of his voice.

"You should have married him, Shirl," Margaret said. "You like the same things."

"Yes, you."

"Me? Shirley, he considers me a nagging wife."

No wonder. But it was not clear that Gregory held any grievance against her to match her litany of complaints about him. She encouraged Margaret's discontent by countering it, telling her she simply didn't appreciate what she had.

"What do I have?"

Gregory, for starters. The children, the house, friends. Margaret need never be alone if she didn't want to, she would need to make an effort not to be surrounded by family and friends. She found this constraining. Shirley almost cried out, imagining herself in Margaret's role.

After the separation, when Margaret mentioned divorce, Shirley expressed shock, reminding her of the indissolubility of marriage.

"Do you really believe that?"

"Yes, I do, and so do you."

"Then how do you explain Frank Sinatra?"

"Frank Sinatra!"

She claimed his marriage had been declared null and void by the Church, as had hundreds of others.

"Are you going to apply for an annulment?"

"Not until after the divorce."

Margaret talked only of Gregory, Gregory talked of his work, and Shirley was fascinated. She would have been fascinated if he had read the Chicago telephone directory to her. But she never for a moment imagined that he regarded her as anything more than an old friend, and an old friend of Margaret's at that. Whatever Margaret might really think of the promises she had made him, Gregory had married her for keeps. Till death do us part.

Margaret visited her in her library office, fooled around with the computer, was fascinated with its desktop publishing capacities. Shirley was glad to show Margaret how she prepared the library newsletter for the printer. And Margaret had written on the screen and stored on the hard disk the legend for her imaginary marriage to Philip Chesney Cord, the legend Shirley had printed and then sent to Sister Mary Teresa.

TWENTY-EIGHT

FOR KATHERINE SENSKI to be unobtrusive was no small feat. Her wide-brimmed hat, her dress, all violet and rose and framed by the black velvet cape she wore with the bravura of a toreador, did not discourage notice. Dark glasses and the magazine behind which she hid would hardly have made her invisible to Shirley Loudon, but then Shirley Loudon was wholly unaware of the outer world as she emerged from Gregory Doyle's shop.

"Laura was right." Katherine sighed half aloud.

"Three ten with tax," the bald boy behind the counter said.

Katherine examined the magazine she had picked up as a shield. *American Voyeur*. The cover informed her of an actress who had been a cat in the seventeenth century, of a grandmother who had become pregnant from eating walnuts, and promised she would find inside recent letters from Elvis.

"And worth every penny," Katherine said, returning it to the rack. "Do you have the *Sacred Heart Messenger?*"

He was rummaging among his wares when she left. She went toward the shop.

"Her friends have stayed his friends," Laura had said, but Katherine detected something in the young reporter's voice.

"Like who?"

"The librarian from the University of Chicago who was a college roommate of his wife."

Katherine tucked in her chin and looked at Laura. "Now, you know her name, Laura. Are you carrying a grudge?"

"Just because of the phony wedding announcement that might have cost me my job? Ha."

"You've kept an eye on her?"

"She is a very frequent presence at Gregory Doyle's shop."

"It's a place of business," Katherine said, knowing that skepticism sharpens the edge of suspicion.

"And he works late."

Katherine sighed and opened her arms as if to embrace the world and all its follies. "Laura, say they have been thrown more closely together by events. Say they have fallen in love even. He is eligible, she is eligible...."

"But when did it start?"

The question conjured up a picture of a love unable to find expression, which could scarcely be acknowledged even in the privacy of Shirley's mind. Katherine pushed away thoughts of her own doomed love affair that had rendered her as celibate as Sister

Mary Teresa. Besides, Laura was developing the most imaginative interpretation of the relation of Shirley Loudon and Gregory Doyle.

"She has loved him all these years, quietly, in the background, while her old friend has the man she loves, bears his children, lives a life of ease. And then wants out."

"Solving Shirley's problems."

"Exactly."

"Are you Catholic?"

"I am."

"Don't you believe that marriage is for life, that divorce is impossible?"

"Yes."

"Gregory Doyle is a Catholic."

"So? Men are weak."

"Laura, I see an affluent future for you as the author of glitzy romances."

But she thought of plain little Shirley Loudon with the beautiful and popular roommate. She imagined Shirley having a crush on Gregory that was not eradicated when Margaret became his fiancée, his wife, the mother of his children. The two women had stayed in touch over the years. Shirley had said their meetings became frequent as Margaret's discontent with her life mounted. Of course she would have seen the rebirth of opportunity in the collapse of the Doyle marriage, she might have subtly encouraged her old friend to seek her real self elsewhere than in her state of life. But so long as Margaret was alive, Gregory would regard her as his wife.

And the puzzling confession of Gregory Doyle was suddenly cast in a new light. Not that Katherine had said it aloud. She would not express such a thought to Laura, she would not even try it out on Emtee Dempsey. But she resolved to see for herself if Laura was right about the relationship between Shirley and Greg. Katherine had just witnessed the third get-together in a week, twice in Doyle's shop, the third when he returned something to the university and they went out for lunch. However Gregory thought of Shirley, it was obvious to Katherine that the librarian was deeply in love with the book dealer. Who was, Katherine was quick to concede, a very attractive man.

"Is there such a thing as a collected works of Willa Cather?" she asked when he came to wait on her.

"There's a uniform edition."

"Do you have it?"

"No, but I could try to find it for you."

"I wonder how much it would be?"

"I wouldn't guess. Anything else?"

"What do you have in stock of Willa Cather's?"

He showed her the American Library volumes and while she was leafing through one said, "You're a reporter, aren't you?"

"What gives me away, my sloping forehead?"

"Someone pointed you out to me."

"Shirley Loudon."

His smile was really very nice. "Why are you spying on me?"

"Perhaps I'm spying on her."

"I don't think I appreciated before what a blessing anonymity is."

"Before you confessed to murder?"

"I admit I brought all this attention on myself. How do I become obscure again?"

Katherine laughed. "By not being so nice to reporters."

She bought the Willa Cather and resolved to leave him alone. The next day, Laura told her Gregory Doyle was having lunch with a young woman.

"You?"

"Irene Maloney."

"She's his lawyer."

"Uh huh. What's he need a lawyer for now?"

"Laura, I think we ought to drop it. All the man wants is privacy."

The echo of her own words in her memory later made her slightly ashamed. Laura was showing the instincts of a reporter and she was discouraging them. Why? Because Gregory Doyle was such an attractive, pleasant man. If she felt that at her age, how much more so Shirley Loudon would. She sat propped up in her bed, Willa Cather ignored on her lap, wondering what Sister Mary Teresa would make of this.

TWENTY-NINE

AT LUNCH GREGORY TOLD Irene of Shirley Loudon's discovery that he was being watched by reporters.

"Who's Shirley Loudon?"

"A friend of my wife's. They were roommates in college."

"She watched the reporters watching you?"

"Maybe they're watching us now."

They had a table about the size of a checkerboard in the crowded dining area of the Ribstone Pippin, famed for its king-size drinks.

"Or queen size, as the case may be."

Irene's manhattan looked as if it could accommodate the whole royal family. "Glad to be back to work?"

"It was awful, sitting in jail, thinking of all the projects I had yet to finish. I suppose dying is like that. Do you know Fitzgerald's notebooks?"

"Fitzgerald? Gregory, I'm just a lawyer."

"I'm confusing you with Shirley."

"Thanks a lot."

He laughed. "I meant the female companionship. Since my troubles with my wife, I've spent an awful lot of time alone. Talking to oneself is overrated. The combination of your favorite speaker and the ideal listener should be unbeatable, but it isn't."

"Isn't Shirley a good listener?"

"She knows a lot of the same things I do."

"Like Fitzgerald?"

"Books. Authors. She's a librarian."

"And I remind you of her?"

"Only when you're mad."

"Who is Fitzgerald?"

He did not speak as an expert witness would, nor did he sound like any teacher she had ever had. A man talking about what he really liked. She must have had some inkling of such things before law school, but they had all become fuzzy and unclear.

"It must be nice to have your business and your interests coincide."

"Are you going to tell me how awful the practice of law is?"

"No! I love it."

They had haddock and dark beer. A cloud of other people's cigarette smoke formed over their table. Normally, she would have reacted in the expected way to the smell of smoke. That very morning she had objected sharply to a man who got onto the elevator still holding a lighted cigarette. Now it seemed fussy and forced to want to interfere with the pleasures of others. He asked if she was engaged.

"Well, at the moment I'm having lunch with a client."

"Speaking of which, I called Benjamin Rush about your bill."

"You didn't."

"Yes, I did. He said to work it out with you."

"All right. I want that book of Fitzgerald's."

"The Crack-up?"

"Is that what it's called?"

She felt always on the verge of making coquettish remarks—reacting to his comparison of her with Shirley Loudon, asking why he cared if she was engaged, and now suggesting that the title seemed ominous. It was important to remember that this man was the father of Bernadette Doyle. He could be *her* father. But then Benjamin Rush could be *his* father and she had a crush on Ben. Young men simply did not interest her. She found herself telling him this, apropos of Benjamin Rush.

"Maybe you have a vocation."

"To what?"

She loved his laughter. "To library science."

"How's Bernadette?"

"What an ordeal I've put her through."

"You? I should think her complaint would be against her mother."

"But none of that was public. At least Bernie has her married name to hide behind."

O'Brien. The Irish still married only the Irish, or was that just Chicago? She took his suggestion and, back at the office, called Bernadette.

"Come out this afternoon and we can play doubles."

"Golf?"

"Tennis!"

"Who with?"

"Two nuns."

"Are you serious?"

"I am. They're good."

"Well, your father suggested I might have a vocation."

THIRTY

THEY PLAYED TWO SETS and then collapsed with iced tea at an umbrella-shaded metal table. Irene Maloney's dark hair lay in wet ringlets on her head, curling over her forehead. Both Bernadette and Joyce looked fresh if flushed. Kim felt as if she might never move again. After a few minutes, Joyce and Bernadette went back onto the court and played singles.

"I belong to a health club," Irene said. "I exercise strenuously at least twice a week. I think I am going to die."

At another table a man sat slouched in a chair, his hand shading his eyes, staring at them. Ignoring him was proving to be difficult.

"I think you have an admirer. Don't look."

"How do I know you're not making him up?"

"Here he comes."

Although he was young, he walked as if he did not want to straighten up entirely. He put his hand on the back of the chair Bernadette had vacated.

"I used to be a Catholic," he said to Kim.

"Oh."

"You're a nun."

"What do you want?" Irene said in a crisp professional voice. He seemed to lay his cheek on his shoulder as he looked at her.

"You one too?"

"One what?"

"Nun. Sister. Religious."

"Are you a member here?"

"Do I look like a member?"

He stood erect then. Above his shirt pocket *Meadowbrook* was embroidered. He turned to display the back of his shirt. GROUNDS.

"You work here." Irene said it as if it were a guess at charades. "Did you have to renounce your religion to get the job?"

He turned away from Irene. "I used to believe it all. Everything. The more fantastic the better. With you it's a job, your life. Right? Of course it is. What are you doing here?"

His voice altered with the question. It was clear that he was shocked to find a nun in tennis shorts spending an afternoon at the Meadowbrook Country Club. Kim was a little shocked herself. But she was here as a matter of obedience as well as pleasure.

"Of course you must go," Emtee Dempsey said, as if an afternoon of tennis were provided for in the rule the Blessed Abigail Keineswegs had written for her daughters in religion.

"Joyce would enjoy it."

"I meant the two of you, of course."

Joyce and Bernadette got along as Kim had been sure they would, trading lore on sports and athletes and tournaments and league standings. Such things stuck effortlessly to Joyce's mind, yet she professed to be astounded by Emtee Dempsey's memory.

"No person of intelligence can be a Christian," their uninvited guest said.

"Do the names Augustine, Ambrose, Anselm, Bonaventure, Aquinas, Dante, and Albert the Great mean anything to you?" Kim asked.

He dismissed this list with a shake of his head. "They lived in a prescientific age."

"All right. How about Descartes, Leibniz, Pascal, Newton, Hobbes, Locke, Milton, Dr. Johnson, Chesterton..." She paused to inhale. "Shall I go on?"

"Do you seriously believe that sometime centuries after you die your dust will be raised up and you'll live again?"

"Yes."

"That's crazy."

"Life would be crazier on the opposite assumption."

"Boris! What are you doing?"

Bernadette came up to the table, and the groundskeeper straightened and turned.

"We're just talking," Kim said.

Bernadette stood looking from Boris to Kim. Finally she said, "You better get back to work."

He studied his watch ostentatiously. "My break is over." He sauntered away, his yellow boots slapping on the patio.

"I'm sorry," Bernadette said. "Was he being a pest?"

"He wanted to talk religion."

"That's what I was afraid of. He's a real kook. But he's a magician in keeping the greens in good shape."

"Do you give up?" Joyce called, and Bernadette trotted back to the court.

"Were all those people you mentioned really believers?"

"Sure. And I'd just started. Can you imagine a Chicago greenskeeper knowing something all those people missed?"

"Do you know a woman named Shirley Loudon?"

"The librarian? She's a graduate of our college."

"So Sister Mary Teresa knows her too?"

"Of course."

Irene fluffed her drying hair and looked to where Joyce had just served an ace. "I think she has a thing for Bernadette's father."

"How so?"

Irene's account of Shirley Loudon's frequent visits to the Doyle bookshop was open to a pretty neutral interpretation. Nonetheless, she told Irene she'd mention it to Emtee Dempsey. The lawyer seemed oddly relieved.

THIRTY-ONE

"THAT'S THE SAME theory Katherine is pushing," Emtee Dempsey said, obviously unimpressed by it.

"What if they've been in love all along?"

"What impediment remained after Margaret left him, after she divorced him? And don't tell me about the indissolubility of the marriage bond. You can't have a man conscientious about that but willing to commit murder in order to get rid of his first wife."

But Kim was not to be put off. How cunning it was for Gregory Doyle to confess to the murder but only when he had arranged for his story to be easily refutable. After all, what had been established other than that he had bought a pair of boots after the murder? "What if he already had another pair?"

At least Emtee Dempsey was listening. The more Kim developed this explanation, the more persuasive she herself found it.

"And say his concern was money, not being free to marry again. Margaret had cost him an awful lot, and she ended up with most of the property. What if money lies behind it all? What if he wanted his property back and he also wanted to keep the manuscript Professor Kotarski had entrusted to him?"

"Others knew he had it. Geoffrey Stone, for one."

"Maybe Stone was next."

"No," she mused. "With Kotarski out of the way he could have contacted the Polish monastery and become their agent for other things."

But the old nun entered into it without enthusiasm. She was confident that Richard and his cohorts would have satisfied themselves that, the boots apart, Gregory Doyle was not an apt candidate for the murder of his wife. Kim was losing her appetite for her theory. She had kept her word to Irene Maloney, whose preference for assassin was clearly Shirley Loudon. Imagining the diminutive librarian killing her old friend and then Professor Kotarski was not easy.

Joyce came in from the kitchen, her step springy. An afternoon on the tennis court had given her a surge of energy rather than the tiredness that made Kim long for bedtime.

"Did you tell Sister about Boris?"

"Boris?" the old nun asked, perking up.

So Kim told the story of the encounter with the apostate groundskeeper at Meadowbrook. If Emtee Dempsey had lent only half an ear to her talk about Shirley Loudon's presumed love for Gregory Doyle, she was wholly alert now. Admittedly, the obnoxious Boris seemed a better candidate as killer of two people, but it seemed completely arbitrary to show such enthusiasm for someone Emtee Dempsey had never even heard of until a few minutes ago.

"Sister Kimberly, this is what I have been looking for! Someone to link the two murders. That is what gave what little plausibility it has to your theory about Gregory Doyle and Shirley Loudon. Boris may very well be the missing link."

"He looks like it," Joyce said, and then tried to seem sorry for having said it.

THIRTY-TWO

THE BOOTS labeled *AO* were in the trunk of the car as Bernadette drove off in answer to Sister Mary Teresa's invitation to come to Walton Street for a talk.

"What's it about?"

"Your mother's murder."

"Oh."

"There's something only you can help me with."

As soon as she agreed and hung up, she thought of a million excuses she might have used to put it off, excuses that could have been renewed indefinitely. She considered calling Kim and begging off, pleading some reason she had not thought of when the old nun called. But she did not pick up the phone again. She felt that what was about to happen had to happen; nothing she might do would prevent it. In the same way, on the drive to Walton Street, she told herself to stop and get rid of the boots in the trunk, put them in a Dumpster, throw them into the weeds beside a remote road. Did she intend to carry the darned things into the house and tell Sister Mary Teresa what their significance was?

Of course she didn't.

But she had to know what the old nun wanted. It was impossible that she'd heard of the incriminating boots that had been found stuck beneath the workbench in the back of the pro shop, Augie's boots.

"I can't find my boots," Augie had said two days before.

"Where did you leave them?" She did not turn to face him as she asked the question.

"That's what I'm trying to think. I thought I left them in the pro shop."

Nothing in his manner suggested that he was concerned beyond the nuisance of not being able to find the boots.

"Use mine."

"Good idea."

A tight fit, but of course he got them on, clambered behind the wheel of his car, and went on a tour of the rain-soaked course. Such a tour gladdened Augie's heart even if Boris clearly resented the implication that his work required any supervision at all. Two elderly maids had rooms under the roof of the clubhouse on the same hallway as Boris, and they routinely complained about the exotic dishes he left simmering on a hot plate throughout the day so that they would have reached a peak of piquancy when he sat down to eat. He was impervious to complaints, completely uncaring about any pain or annoyance he might cause others. He had his own grievances to brood over.

"The faculty is all socialists and communists," he groused in explanation of his brief career as a graduate student.

"All?" Augie asked. Bernie had pleaded with him not to egg Boris on, but he found it impossible to resist.

"They didn't accept the credits I earned in Lublin."

"Maybe they think you're a Catholic."

Boris had seized upon this as a possible ironic explanation of his thwarted academic career. He composed a letter in which he abjured and denounced the Christian faith and all its works and pomps. He sent it to each member of the history department. A week later he telephoned the departmental secretary to see if the letter had arrived and was put on hold. His fury mounted as he listened to Muzak. He waited ten minutes and then cursed the poor woman in Polish. She hung up on him. All this fitted into his conviction that the University of Chicago was frightened of him. He was composing an op-ed piece detailing his case against the university.

"That ought to do it," Augie said.

Boris missed the irony but found encouragement unacceptable in any case. The prospect of success conflicted with his theory of the universe and his place in it.

"Tell me all about Boris," Sister Mary Teresa said before Bernadette was settled into the chair across the desk from the old nun.

"Boris!"

"Boris."

She could have cried with relief. Kim looked sheepish.

"Bernie, I told Sister Mary Teresa about my encounter with him."

But the little nun dismissed such distractions, launching immediately into the questions she wished to put to Bernadette. First, did her father visit her at Meadowbrook? Did he talk to her of his shop, of the work he was doing? Bernadette nodded.

"Had he told you of the thirteenth-century Polish manuscript he was working on?"

"He mentioned it, yes."

"And this was before your mother's death?"

She had to think, but of course it had to be. That visit was very different from the several he had paid them since all the trouble began.

"Good. Now, remember that visit as carefully as you can. When and where, precisely, did he mention that manuscript to you?"

"Sister, it wasn't any kind of dramatic announcement. But I knew of it, I learned of it from him, we were just sitting having a beer—"

"Where?"

This was the last thing Bernadette had expected on the drive to Walton Street. Along with the relief she felt came the sense that she was failing some important examination. She looked at Kim.

"We were at one of the tables on the patio. Not far from where we had iced tea today."

The old nun turned to Kim and asked for, and got, a detailed picture of the clubhouse on its slight hill, the course spread out below it, to the east the swimming pool, to the west the tennis courts, and the great arc of a patio on which stood clusters of shaded tables where members had drinks or whatever throughout the day. Waiters and waitresses swooped down on tables as soon as they were occupied. Bernadette felt she was seeing her daily circumstances in a bright new light as Kim described them.

"Waiters and waitresses."

Sister Mary Teresa frowned. She shook them away as a distraction. "Now, can you remember yourself seated at that table as your father, however casually, told you of this medieval manuscript he had been asked to restore?"

And she could. She and Augie were there with her dad, who neither golfed nor played tennis. They had persuaded him to have a beer. He was very curious about their life, their work, the details of their day. It was what her father had called the lugubrious presence of Boris that had prompted his mention of the manuscript. With proletarian resentment, Boris had flung himself down at the table next to theirs and seethed because he was not waited on. When he gestured toward the waitress he seemed to be displaying the great damp stain under his arm. Augie had mentioned that Boris was a thwarted scholar. Polish. And that had set her father off.

Emtee Dempsey glowed with delight as she heard this. Her pudgy little hands were steepled and her face shone over them like the rising sun.

"Could Boris have heard?"

It was impossible to sit on the patio and be unaware of the talk at nearby tables. "I suppose."

The little hands parted and then came soundlessly together. "Perfect!"

What the old nun had been searching for, and now thought she had in Boris, was a link between the two murders.

"How have things been left by the police? Your mother is surprised by a burglar and cruelly slain. Some weeks later, Professor Kotarski is surprised by a burglar and is senselessly killed. Two unpremeditated and unrelated killings. Perhaps. It is not logically impossible. But I refuse to accept it. And now

I know why. What is the obvious similarity between those two terrible killings?''

She looked brightly from Kim to Bernadette. Bernie took her cue from Kim and remained silent.

''What neither burglar found!'' She lifted slightly from her chair. ''Your mother's room was torn apart but nothing was missing. The thief had searched for something he did not find. Professor Kotarski's rooms were a shambles. Once more the thief hunted for what was not there. Only this time, we know what he was looking for. The manuscript! The invaluable medieval document that the *Tribune* told all Chicago about after the to-do at the jail when Professor Kotarski insisted on seeing your father. The thief who broke into your mother's house and killed her when she surprised him was looking for the same thing. And he was the same man.''

She sat back, but she did not relax.

''Why would he think my mother had it?''

''Because she was your mother. Would Boris be aware of your parents' separation and divorce?''

''I don't know.'' Was that—or, at least, had that— been common knowledge before her mother's murder?

''In the telephone directory, the only entry for Gregory Doyle is the house in which your mother lived. The Bibliothèque Doyle is in the business section, and his private number is given with that entry."

"And you think Boris assumed my father had it at the house...."

The old nun frowned at the use of "assumed." "Very well, call it an assumption, a hypothesis, a theory. However called, we must put it to the test."

"How?"

"That is why I asked you to come here, Bernadette. I want you to take part in something which will flush our thief." Her brow darkened. "Our murderer."

THIRTY-THREE

KATHERINE SENSKI was pulled between loyalty to Sister Mary Teresa and her instinctive feeling that her old friend was grasping at straws and courting disaster. She told herself that if she were truly loyal she would prevent Emtee Dempsey from making a fool out of herself by confronting her old friend with all the obvious objections to her speculation about Boris, the Meadowbrook groundskeeper. But when she brought herself to say something, she found herself drawn deeply into the scheme.

"I shall need reliable information as to the man's whereabouts at the crucial times."

"The police will not reopen their investigation."

"I was not thinking of the police."

So Katherine talked to Laura Cousins, who interviewed the two maids who lived on the top floor of the clubhouse and shared a hallway with Boris Pryzwyaski. She checked with the man in charge of the shed where maintenance vehicles were kept and found that Boris had borrowed a jeep and been absent at the relevant times.

"Do you trust your source?" Katherine asked Laura.

"Boris had to sign out and sign in. I saw the records."

Sister Mary Teresa said she would telephone Laura and thank her personally for this essential information. Katherine's doubts about the old nun began to fade. "Now you have something to show the police."

The blue eyes found the exact center of the round lenses of her gold-rimmed spectacles. "There are other things to do before we bring in Richard Moriarity."

What she had in mind was to set a trap. She had already begun to put her plan in motion. Bernadette had been sent back to Meadowbrook with specific instructions on how to bait the trap.

Kim said, "She will allow Boris to overhear her talking of the manuscript."

"Enticing him to make a third try?"

Kim nodded, but it bothered Katherine that the young nun avoided looking her directly in the eye. Did she have similar misgivings about what Emtee Dempsey was up to?

"You are leading him into temptation, Sister Mary Teresa."

"If he prays the Lord's Prayer sincerely he will resist it."

"When he learns it is in a vault, he won't make another try."

"I think you're right."

"Sister, if he is merely caught in Gregory Doyle's shop—"

"Oh, I have no intention of sending him there."

"Where then?"

"Here."

No wonder Kim wouldn't meet her eyes. The best one could hope for was that the initial premise of the whole enterprise was false and Boris would not show up. If he did, if he had indeed murdered two people in unsuccessful attempts to lay his hands on that manuscript, he would be a mortal menace in the house on Walton Street.

"What is he like?" Katherine asked.

"Crazy."

"Crazy! Are you serious?"

Kim told of the groundskeeper's visit to the table at which she and Irene Maloney were sitting. What would such a man do if he were lured to Walton Street and found once again that the manuscript was not where he had thought it was?

"Oh, but it will be. I intend to have it here."

Katherine decided to do what she could to scuttle Emtee Dempsey's plan. She would feel like a rat, it would be devastating to their friendship if the old nun discovered what she was doing, but the more

Katherine thought of it the clearer it was to her that the best way to be a friend to her old friend was to become temporarily her enemy.

"Will Gregory Doyle agree to that?"

"We shall see. Sister Kimberly and I intend to pay him a visit."

"You are going to his store!"

"Why are you astonished?"

"Why? Apart from your morning trip to the cathedral, how often do you leave this house?"

"Whenever doing so is imperative if I am to walk faithfully in the vocation to which I have been called."

"That sounds like a quotation."

"Don't be facetious, Katherine."

When she left, Katherine drew Kim out onto the front porch. "You can't let her do this, Kim."

"You heard what she said." Sister Kimberly's unwavering loyalty to Emtee Dempsey was edifyingly annoying.

"Who was she quoting?"

"Whom. Oh, I'm sorry. I even sound like her."

"Hume," Katherine mused. "David?"

"Don't be facetious, Katherine."

"You're right. You do sound like her."

THIRTY-FOUR

GEOFFREY STONE SAT in Gregory Doyle's work-room and thought of all the people who, if they saw him in this setting, would deny the testimony of their eyes. The workbench, the presses, the paraphernalia of Doyle's trade, all that was one thing, but dominating the room was a little old nun wearing the kind of habit one only saw in television commercials or condescending films that proved the old adage that anti-Catholicism is the anti-Semitism of the liberal. Stone realized that the embarrassment he felt at the thought of being seen with Sister Mary Teresa had not occurred to him when he saw her in her native setting. But now the incredible starched headgear that brought memories of the paper planes of his youth filled him with incredulity that such a woman actually existed.

Not only existed but, as he knew full well, had a well-earned reputation as a historian and who was at the moment clearly in charge. Even Lavinia, the maid, her dusting wand hanging at her side, followed with wide eyes and wider mouth what Sister Mary Teresa was saying.

"No, Gregory, that won't do. Mere pretense will not do. We must use the manuscript itself." She joined her hands. "I know Professor Kotarski would want us to."

Stone doubted that, but even if he didn't doubt it he would have thought it foolish in the extreme to test the old nun's theories about what had happened to Joseph and to Doyle's former wife by using an invaluable medieval manuscript as bait. Quite apart from the risk that it might actually be stolen if things went awry, carting it about and subjecting it to unnecessary and significant temperature changes endangered it. Doyle had elaborate temperature control equipment in his vault and could seal off his workroom and equalize the temperature and humidity before bringing such a delicate artifact from the vault to his workbench.

Sister Kimberly, the young nun, sat beside Sister Mary Teresa, an enigmatic smile on her face. Stone somehow found it strange that a nun should be a redhead, and a good-looking one at that. Katherine Senski and Laura Cousins sat opposite Stone and next to Bernadette Doyle.

"My insurance would not cover the manuscript if I took it out of the store for such a purpose, Sister. If anything happened, I would be personally liable."

"Mr. Rush?" the old nun said to the distinguished white-haired lawyer for whom they had waited before beginning, since Sister Mary Teresa insisted he had to be there. Stone doubted if Doyle had ever before had half as many people in his workroom together.

"I should think that is quite true."

"Could we insure it for the time it is at Walton Street?"

Rush, incredibly, agreed to look into this, and then she was addressing him.

"Professor Stone, how had you planned to protect the manuscript when Professor Kotarski brought it to the Newberry on the occasion of his lecture?"

"The question never arose."

"Of course it didn't. Professor Kotarski had the manuscript in his possession prior to bringing it here. I doubt that he had taken out some special insurance policy."

If the others found this odd, Stone did not. What was such a policy supposed to assure the insurer in the event of the loss of the manuscript? It could not be replaced. Monetary compensation could never alter that simple and devastating fact. Doyle had crossed the room to speak to Lavinia, who, roused from her rapt eavesdropping, went into the bookstore, closing the door behind her.

"The same can be said of life insurance," the old nun replied when he formulated this thought. "In any case, I shall take responsibility and Mr. Rush will look into insuring it."

"Stone makes the important point," Doyle said. "If the manuscript is lost, no amount of money could make up for the loss."

The old nun turned to him. "Professor Stone and I owe a special debt to Professor Kotarski. He had promised to take part in a lecture series organized by Professor Stone, and there is no doubt that his presentation would have created a sensation. He intended to announce his finding of the manuscript and to allow the assembled scholars at least a fleeting and preliminary glance at it. That intention suggests his attitude toward his discovery. It did not belong to him. It was not something he could enjoy in solitude. It was a common good, and a common good is meant to be shared and enjoyed. Professor Stone will agree with me that the small risk to the manuscript my proposal involves is more than offset by the opportunity of finding the slayer of Professor Kotarski."

Stone found her description of Kotarski's attitude toward the manuscript so completely out of whack with Kotarski's miserly possessiveness that he could not believe she was serious. His surprise undid him, his hesitation was taken as acquiescence, and the old

nun and Doyle were soon discussing the logistics of
transferring the manuscript to the house on Walton
Street.

"Why aren't the police represented here?" Stone
asked.

"Sister Kimberly," the old nun said, dipping one
wing of her headdress toward her companion. The
young nun said that she would be going from this
meeting downtown where she would speak to Inspector Richard Moriarity.

"Her brother," Katherine Senski said.

Stone's objection to the project had been mild to
begin with. He found the old nun's theory that the
two murders were related to an attempt to steal the
manuscript fantastic. Of course whoever killed Kotarski was looking for the manuscript, but linking
that to the killing of Mrs. Doyle made no sense. Boris
Pryzwyaski sounded like someone the nuns had in-
vented. As far as he was concerned, if the police were
in on it, he would not oppose the testing of the old
nun's theory. After it had been disproved, he could
resume thinking how he could possibly cut himself in
on the money Kotarski's manuscript would bring at
auction.

After the meeting broke up, the two reporters
commandeered Gregory Doyle. Stone exchanged
banalities with Bernadette O'Brien and then went out
into the bookstore where Sister Mary Teresa was

chatting with Lavinia while Sister Kimberly browsed. Stone pushed through the door and into the street and wondered if anyone noticed that he had left or even cared.

THIRTY-FIVE

THE FOLLOWING NIGHT Kim drove the VW bug to the Bibliothèque Doyle as arranged. When she got to the shopping center, she took the outer drive, which brought her around to the loading ramp at the rear of the store. She flashed her lights as she approached, and before the VW came to a stop the metal door began to lift and soon Gregory Doyle appeared, silhouetted against the illuminated interior of his storage room. He then walked along the dock, climbed down a ladder to the level of the parking lot, and came to the passenger door of the VW. Kim reached across and opened the door. He put the wrapped package on the seat before looking at her.

"It's all yours."

"It'll be safe."

Like him she had to take on faith that her every movement was under the scrutiny of the police. She had detected no sign of surveillance when she left Walton Street; on the drive over she had noticed no unmarked car following her; now she and Doyle might have been the only two persons left on earth.

The motor of the VW sounded preternaturally loud in the night.

The drive back to Walton Street was uneventful, although the sense of being alone in the world did not survive the heavy traffic Kim had to negotiate. At intersections, cars pulled even with her on either side and she glanced now right, now left, half hoping to surprise some sign that the driver was her guardian angel.

She parked in front of the house and Joyce had the front door open before Kim crossed the sidewalk. She skipped up the steps and inside. Behind her, as she went down the hall, Joyce locked the front door. Kim took the package into the study and placed it on the desk in front of Sister Mary Teresa.

"Thank you, Sister."

"Are you going to open it?"

"In a moment. Before you leave, raise the blind of that window."

"Why don't I stay here with you? My presence wouldn't dissuade anyone."

But the great headdress swayed negatively. "We will do just as we planned."

So Kim raised the venetian blinds and separated the drapes of the window, the better to provide a clear view to an outside observer of the old nun at her desk as she unwrapped the package and set about studying the precious thirteenth-century manuscript. The stage was set. The trap was baited.

Richard, Gleason, and O'Connell were on vigil in the house, the two detectives upstairs, Richard in the darkened kitchen, sipping coffee. Kim went downstairs to the basement apartment where Katherine, Laura Cousins, and Lavinia awaited. Asking the woman who cleaned up the Bibliothèque Doyle had been one of Emtee Dempsey's surprises.

"I think she may be of help."

"To clean up the house after the shoot-out?"

Emtee Dempsey dipped her head and trained a blue eye on Kim. "I understand that passengers boarding airplanes are arrested if they joke about the danger of the coming flight."

"I think you're right." But Kim took the old nun's point. She and Joyce like Emtee Dempsey were to radiate confidence in what they were doing and above all to discourage any notion that danger was involved.

"He seems to prefer heavy and cheap objects rather than guns," Richard said cheerfully. "I am beginning to see the practical value of the habit." He looked piously at Kim and Joyce. "To say nothing of its religious significance."

In the basement apartment, Katherine was smoking a cigarette she had borrowed from Laura. Lavinia sat in front of the all but inaudible TV. Kim told her to turn up the sound a bit.

"I can read their lips," Lavinia said.

"Ah, a Republican." Katherine launched a perfect smoke ring, and Kim could see that Joyce was sorely tempted to have a cigarette herself. Not that she would, with witnesses.

They all spoke in whispers, and Kim began to pick up the voices of the televised drama Lavinia was watching. The cleaning lady was as wide as she was high, and she sat sidesaddle on a hassock as if ready to leap to her feet at the sound of an approaching employer. Joyce had brought Lavinia a beer, which she had gladly taken, though refusing a glass to drink it from.

"I don't want to dirty no dishes."

Did she think she'd have to wash them? Joyce had asked if Emtee Dempsey was thinking of engaging Lavinia for a day each week, the cleaning lady's usual arrangement. Joyce seemed to have mixed feelings about the prospect. The explanation was far simpler. Lavinia had gone once a week to the Doyle home before the separation; her arrangements after the Doyles had parted was a day at the house, a day at the store. Kim suspected that Emtee Dempsey had more interest in quizzing the cleaning lady about her original place of employment.

The whispers died away as time passed and they became more conscious of the fact that they were waiting. It was now nine o'clock. When would he come? Katherine was wearing a cloak, although the basement apartment was as comfortable as any other place in the house; she had wrapped it about her and settled into a corner of a couch, clearly expecting a long wait.

"If he comes at all."

Kim could almost imagine Katherine crossing her fingers, superstitiously expressing the opposite of what she hoped. Laura had a laptop computer with her, and from time to time turned it on and tapped away on its keyboard, perhaps making notes for the story she hoped would emerge from this adventure. Kim found herself thinking of the old nun, upstairs in her study, visible from the street as she worked at her desk. Bernadette was to have made sure that Boris knew the manuscript was at Walton Street, and if he made an attempt to steal it, the presumption would be that he was the man responsible for the deaths of Margaret Doyle and Professor Kotarski. In the increasingly silent though restless basement apartment, this theory seemed farfetched and their vigil doomed to disappointment.

The ringing telephone brought them all to the edges of their chairs. Lavinia turned clockwise on the hassock. All eyes were on the telephone. In the middle of the second ring it stopped. Emtee Dempsey would have answered it in the study. Kim got up and went to the bottom of the stairs. Richard was visible, the phone pressed to his ear, his hand over the receiver. As Kim watched, he took the phone from his ear and moved away from the door. Kim went up.

"Who was it?"

"Bernadette O'Brien. He just left the club."

"Boris?"

"Who we talking about, Batman?"

Kim could have cheered. Emtee Dempsey was right after all! She started toward the study, but Richard stopped her.

"Why don't we just keep to the script?"

Meaning, not to alert anyone watching the old nun at her desk that the house was full of police, reporters, other nuns. If Boris had just left Meadowbrook, it would be half an hour at least before he showed up. Nonetheless, Richard was right. Besides, Emtee Dempsey would have scolded her if she had looked into the study now. Kim opened the refrigerator and took out a beer.

"Want one?"

"Not now. Who's that for?"

"Lavinia."

Kim would not have admitted it to Richard, but she had the fleeting thought that Lavinia was a good luck charm, that somehow her presence in the house was influencing the outcome of the plan Emtee Dempsey had set in motion.

Half an hour passed and the house seemed to grow more silent. The traffic outside on Walton Street came to them as an uninterrupted, undifferentiated hum. A lull seemed to come even in that. There had been ample time for Boris to drive from Meadowbrook. Something had to happen soon. This unspoken thought increased the tension, and Kim could feel an edgy impatience mix with the excitement. Why didn't he come!

Forty-five minutes, then a full hour passed since the call from Bernadette. Kim went to the bottom of the stairs, then mounted them soundlessly, one at a time. When she came into the kitchen, Richard was not there. She had the crazy thought that the house was empty, that they had been sitting downstairs in the basement apartment, quiet as mice, and everyone else was gone. What in the name of God had happened? She held her breath and the sound of her heart was like a drumbeat in her ears as she crept down the hall to the study.

"Kim!"

A scream escaped her throat and she actually jumped as she wheeled and turned. Richard!

"You nearly scared me to death."

"What are you sneaking around for?" He took her hand and led her back to the kitchen.

"Hasn't he come?"

"This was a damn fool idea in the first place."

"Oh, was it? Then why are you here?"

From the study came a very audible, "Shhhhhhh."

Richard raised his eyes. He whispered. "She insists that everything is going fine."

The phone rang and Richard leapt to it, waited for the ring to be interrupted, and lifted the instrument to his ear. Kim did not at all like the expression that spread over his face. He held the phone toward her and Kim could make out female voices, Sister Mary Teresa and, she supposed, Bernadette's.

"Boris has returned to Meadowbrook," Richard said.

He started for the doorway, apparently intent on striding down to the study, when the receiver he wore strapped to his belt gave off a warning buzz. That would be from O'Connell or Gleason, upstairs. Richard stepped back into the kitchen and held up his hand. There was a probing sound in the front door lock. Richard motioned for Kim to go back downstairs, but she felt she couldn't move. Even if she could, she had no intention of going.

How eerily the metallic sound carried through the house as someone on the porch worked on the front door lock. Then the lock turned, followed by the familiar squeak of the door opening. There was the sound of swift movement down the hallway.

"Good evening, young man," Sister Mary Teresa said in a loud voice in which there was not a trace of fear. "I have been expecting you."

Richard had pressed buttons on his transceiver as soon as the door opened, and now he went on the run down the hallway. Kim followed, but she was pushed aside by Gleason and O'Connell, who had thundered down from upstairs. By the time Kim managed to wedge her way into the study, the intruder was in handcuffs. He looked from face to face with wide, startled, hating eyes. Richard was reciting to the man from a card in what might have been a liturgical ceremony. Now from downstairs the rest of them came, but it was Lavinia's remark that wrote finis to the evening.

"Billy!" she cried, at the sight of the intruder. "Billy, what in the world you doing here?"

THIRTY-SIX

THAT BILLY, the boyfriend of Virgie, a cleaning lady friend of Lavinia, should prove to be the missing link between the murders of Margaret Nelson Doyle and Professor Kotarski had occurred to Sister Mary Teresa only when they were assembled at the Bibliothèque Doyle preparing to set a trap for Boris.

"We have the bad habit of ignoring the existence of people like Lavinia as they do their jobs about us. We speak as if they were not there."

Gregory Doyle nodded. "Of course she would have heard me speak of the manuscript. She was here on the occasion of Professor Kotarski's first visit. It never occurred to me that she was listening or would understand if she were."

And what do cleaning ladies talk about when they get together? Those whose places they clean. It was in the natural course of events that Lavinia should have told her friend Virgie and that Virgie should mention it to her *fainéant* boyfriend.

"What kind of boyfriend?" Richard asked, trying to make the best of this.

"Ne'er-do-well."

"He's got a record as long as your arm." And then, considering the length of Sister Mary Teresa's arm, Richard looked as if he might substitute another metaphor. "His girlfriend didn't realize she was feeding him information. Half a dozen break-ins as well as the murders can be traced to information Billy got from Virgie."

"She mustn't blame herself," Emtee Dempsey said.

"She doesn't. She blames you."

"Me!"

"For setting Billy up."

Billy of course denied everything. He would doubtless deny breaking into the house on Walton Street.

"Why did he break into Margaret Doyle's place?"

"The information he got did not include the fact that the Doyles are divorced. The only telephone directory entry for Gregory Doyle is the house on North Shore. Virgie would have told him that Lavinia worked there; he assumed that's where the manuscript was; poor Margaret surprised him as he searched."

"And Katherine alerted him to the owner of the manuscript."

Katherine did not rise to Richard's teasing. "What a trail of ineptitude the man made."

Joyce said, "I was counting on Boris."

"Where had he gone on all those occasions he left Meadowbrook?"

"He is taking a night course at Roosevelt University."

"History?"

"World religions."

"He would be better advised to look into an other-worldly one," Emtee Dempsey murmured.

And that seemed to be that. Richard behaved well, but then he could rightly claim that he and Emtee Dempsey had set the trap into which Billy walked.

"I still think she was waiting for Boris," he said to Kim.

No need to answer. He might be right. But how then to explain Emtee Dempsey's inviting Lavinia to the vigil on Walton Street? Irene Maloney stopped by to congratulate Sister Mary Teresa, and Bernadette O'Brien and her husband Augie came too. They were closeted with the old nun in the study and Bernie's eyes were red when they emerged. The poor woman. It was easy at this moment of triumph to forget that she had lost her mother.

Two days later, when they were at prayer in the chapel, Kim's eyes popped open. What about the boot mark made in the spilled talcum powder in Margaret Doyle's bedroom? Once the question occurred to her, she was unable to concentrate, and there were fifteen minutes remaining before they would leave the chapel for the dinner table. Kim offered it up, mocked herself for finding it so difficult to endure the waiting. This was a question she had to put to Sister Mary Teresa. She was glad she hadn't thought of it when Richard was in the house. Here was a loose end unaccounted for by Emtee Dempsey's triumph.

At table, Kim actually waited until after the main course before bringing it up. She imagined merit for self-denial accruing to her account in heaven. Then Joyce served the mince pie and coffee.

"It's a good thing no one thought of the boot print in Margaret Doyle's bedroom," she said casually, pouring cream into her coffee.

"No one?"

"Oh, you can explain that?"

"It would be more accurate to say that I have been given the explanation."

"What is it?" Joyce asked from the kitchen doorway, where she had come to a stop at Kim's question.

"Bernadette thought her father suspected her of making that boot print. Nonsense, of course. There was no need to conceal her presence in the bedroom. Later she came to suspect what her father had."

"What?"

"That it was Augie O'Brien's boot print."

Emtee Dempsey set her great headdress in motion as she thought of the ways of men and women. She brought her coffee cup carefully over her starched wimple, little finger extended, and sipped. She returned her cup to its saucer.

"Well?" Joyce said.

Emtee Dempsey seemed surprised that Joyce and Kim were waiting for more. Kim said, "*Was* it his boot print?"

"Of course. And poor Bernadette suffered agony thinking that her own husband had killed her mother. Even after the explanation became known, she fretted over that boot print." She sat back and closed her eyes, letting the thought form. "That boot print was the seal of spousal love." She opened her eyes. "He followed her to the house when Margaret called her and, when she came sprinting out again, went inside to see what had terrified her."

"Why didn't he say anything?"

"He did. He told me just two days ago, when the two of them were here."

"Before. Why didn't he speak up before?"

"To what end?" the old nun asked, rising from the table, signaling the end of the meal and of the conversation. Her tiny hand traced over her starched bosom the sign of the cross and she bowed her head to give thanks, leaving the question to the future ruminations of the young nuns.

APPEARANCE OF EVIL
Carolyn Coker
An Andrea Perkins Mystery

THE FINE ART OF MURDER

As houseguest of one of the Huntington Museum's board members, art restorer Andrea Perkins is dimly aware of the discovery of a corpse on the grounds of the museum.

LAPD detectives Roberson and Lopez, however, are very involved, exploring a connection between the dead body— and the acts of a graffiti artist who is spraying garish clothes on the statues.

But when the search for the killer begins to involve Andrea's hostess, Andrea must confront a disturbing appearance of evil that even wealth and beauty cannot hide.

"Top-notch characterization..."—*Publishers Weekly*

Available in December at your favorite retail stores.

Into a world where danger lurks around
every corner, and there's a fine line between trust
and betrayal, comes a tall, dark and handsome man.

Intuition draws you to him…but instinct keeps you
away. Is he really one of those…

You made the dozen "Dangerous Men" from 1995 so
popular that there's a sextet of these sexy but
secretive men coming to you in 1996!

In January, look for:

#353 OUTLAWED!
by B. J. Daniels

Take a walk on the wild side…with our
"DANGEROUS MEN"!

CRIMINALS ALWAYS HAVE SOMETHING TO HIDE—BUT THE ENJOYMENT YOU'LL GET OUT OF A WORLDWIDE MYSTERY NOVEL IS NO SECRET....

With Worldwide Mystery on the case, we've taken the mystery out of finding something good to read every month.

Worldwide Mystery is guaranteed to have suspense buffs and chill seekers of all persuasions in eager pursuit of each new exciting title!

Worldwide Mystery novels—crimes worth investigating...

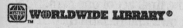 **WORLDWIDE LIBRARY®**

WWMGEN

New York Times Bestselling Author

PENNY JORDAN

Explore the lives of four women as they overcome a

CRUEL LEGACY

For Philippa, Sally, Elizabeth and Deborah life will never be the same after the final act of one man. Now they must stand on their own and reclaim their lives.

As Philippa learns to live without wealth and social standing, Sally finds herself tempted by a man who is not her husband. And Elizabeth struggles between supporting her husband and proclaiming her independence, while Deborah must choose between a jealous lover and a ruthless boss.

Don't miss CRUEL LEGACY, available this December at your favorite retail outlet.

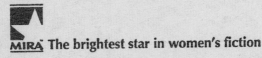 **MIRA** The brightest star in women's fiction

MPJCL